"Kathy Fish's *Together We Can Bury It* is a wonder—stories filled with sadness, humor, and longing—a slanted banged-up beauty of a world that feels like this one, only more."

—Jeff Landon, author of *Emily Avenue*

"Full of grace and wit, Kathy Fish's *Together We Can Bury It* takes one to the familiar, yet bizarre: worlds of wonder, ache, and hope. Worlds not to forget. A refreshing voice, busting of compassion, guts, and wisdom. This collection shines with amazing delight."

—Kim Chinquee, author of *Oh Baby*

"There's a movie's worth of character and plot and insight in every blooming one of these short fictions. I finished this book feeling stuffed, dazed, and amazed by how much Kathy Fish gets done in such tight spaces. It's a thrill to be privy to what she thinks about, the wonder she carries inside."

—Pia Z. Ehrhardt, author of *Famous Fathers*

TOGETHER
WE CAN BURY IT

kathy fish

TOGETHER
WE CAN BURY IT

THE LIT PUB
thelitpub.com

Cover art and design by Jana Vukovic.
Prepress by sunnyoutside.

ISBN: 978-1-937662-04-2
Second edition.

Thank you to the editors of the following publications where some of these fictions first appeared: "Foreign Film" in *Cranky*; "Fine Girl" in *Dark Sky Magazine*; "The Hollow" in *The Denver Quarterly*; "Movement" in *Everyday Genius*; "Wren," "Maidenhead to Oxford," "Baby, Baby," "Wild Yellow Dog, Giant Red Fox" and "Blooms" in *FRiGG*; "Lens" in *Ghoti*; "Disassembly" in *Guernica*; "Blooms" in *Indiana Review*; "Authentic Smorgasbord Dinner" and "Wake Up" in *Juked*; "Empty," "Space Man," "Be My, Be My Baby" and "Tails" in *Keyhole*; "Rodney & Chelsea" in *Mississippi Review* online; "Skinny Lullaby At the Lizard Lounge: Schenectady" and "Cure" in *Necessary Fiction*; "Snow" in *New South*; "Another Story About Me and Some Guy," "Moro," and "What Kind of Person Gives Secrets to the Sky" in *Night Train*; "Lip" in *PANK*; "Cancer Arm" in *Per Contra*; "Watermelon" in *Quick Fiction*; "Night at the Reservoir on Airline Drive" in *Slice*; "Repair Man," "Florida," "Tenderoni," and "Daffodil" in *SmokeLong Quarterly*; "Repair Man" and "Searching for Samuel Beckett" in *Spork*; "Breathless" in *Staccato Fiction*; "Orlando" in *Storyglossia*; "Moth Woman" in *Unmoveable Feast*; "Swicks Rule!" in *Wigleaf*; "Shoebox" in *Wild Strawberries*; and "See Jane" in *Willows Wept Review*. "Foreign

Film," "Shoebox," "The Hollow," "Lens," "This Is Dwight," and "What Kind of Person Gives Secrets to the Sky?" also appeared in *A Particular Feeling of Restlessness* (Rose Metal Press, 2008); and "Watermelon," "Tenderoni," "Space Man," "Disassembly," and "Cancer Arm" also appeared in *Wild Life* (Matter Press, 2010).

For my family.
For everyone that I love.

Contents

I.
*The subtitles flash
in quick succession.*

SEE JANE

When Jane was greedy, her mother would say she had a little pink pig inside her. All you do is want and take, Sweetie, she said. They moved into a new house when Jane started high school. A bigger one they could all fit into, in a better neighborhood. But Jane liked the old house better. The clapboard with the cave basement and one bathroom and a toilet between her bedroom and the kitchen and that steep staircase that everyone had fallen down, then dreamed of falling down, and that attic the birds could get into and fly, fly down the staircase and into the living room and slam into the walls and that back porch and that garden and that crab apple tree and that incinerator on the block and those morning glories blooming on that back fence and the rhubarb and the hollyhocks and the neighbor girl with braces on her legs who came around collecting for Easter Seals. Once, Jane watched her mother remove her wedding ring with butter. She watched her fix her hat and her lipstick and walk out the door. And later, she watched her father push her mother into the lime green wall and Jane ran and came back, ran and came back, until she grew up and rode a train through the snow to Chicago and drank whiskey sours and gimlets, tipping the glass under a veil she wore over her face.

FOREIGN FILM

They are watching a movie about a man who cheats on his wife, whom he loves, and is so disconsolate that his wife eventually loses all patience and leaves him. They are at the point in the film where the man considers his many blunders as he walks along a rocky shoreline carrying what looks to be a large vase. The director of the film is Yugoslavian.

They have argued through dinner and through the night and now it's nearly dawn. They have no eyes for subtitles. The musical score unnerves them. It is exactly the sound of an accordion squeezing the life out of a kitten.

The woman rolls off the couch and lies on the floor. The light in the room changes. Through the window, the clouds resemble dove's feathers. The man stretches his legs. He mutes the television and chuckles. She thinks he muted the television to make sure she would hear him chuckle.

"I'm going out there," she says, pointing. "I'm going to put my boots on and go for a walk."

The disconsolate man's face fills the screen but the couple is no longer watching. The subtitles flash in quick succession.

"And when I get back, I'm taking a shower," she continues. "And you, Laughing Man, you can do whatever you want."

The man in the film stares. The screen is clear of words. His gaze is urgent and equable.

"Are you listening to me?" she asks. She has not gotten up. She has not put on her boots.

"It's all here," he says, tapping his forehead. "It's been archived." He chuckles again, eyes closed.

The room brightens. She stands and hovers over him. He is sleeping. She splays the fingers of one hand and lowers them to his face. The click and whoosh of the furnace makes her jump. She turns to the television. The disconsolate man has waded into the surf. He cocks the vase back in his palm and heaves it in a wide arc into the sea.

REPAIR MAN

The repairman dreams in black and white of cogs and band saws, electrical circuits and wires. When he wakes, he recalls that he was once an old man. He says, Mattie I'm frightened, and she coos to him, brings milk.

He works making repairs for the subway system. Mattie says his work clothes require industrial strength. He takes them to the Wife Saver Laundromat in the retail strip near their apartment building. The repairman is studying to be a transportation engineer. He likes working underground, where it's dark and cool, but the bills are piling up. Nights, Mattie reads and rereads the texts aloud for him, her feet propped on the kitchen table. She runs a yellow highlighter over key points.

After, they wrangle under the covers, the streetlight shining through their one, tiny window. The repairman is conscientious in this as he is with all things, light with his fingers and his tongue. His hair falls over his eyes as he works her.

He knows that someday Mattie will take to calling him Handsome Mole. That her skin will never wrinkle. That she will someday board a train with faulty brakes. He knows, but he is helpless to change things. The repairman will someday carry a backpack full of books to the Wife Saver but he will fail to open them. He'll say, Mattie I'm frightened, but she won't coo to him. And he will die alone on an ice morning, walking past the subway to church.

SNOW

The snow started late Friday afternoon and every-one struggled driving home. Cars moved fune-really up the cul-de-sac, turning into driveways, into garage doors opening like mouths. It snowed through the night while the people slept and they woke to ten inches and it was still coming down, drifting and swirling now, up against the north sides of the houses and the fences and you could only see the smoke coming from the chimneys and the muffled, jaundiced light from the windows. No-body emerged, no garage doors opened, even the children stayed inside and oh the novelty of it, ev-eryone had prepared and bought treats and snacks and brought home stacks of DVDs from the video store and stayed in their pajamas and played board games and the parents said isn't this great, we're spending time together as a family. Patio tables resembled huge, frosted layer cakes and second story windows were blocked from the snow on the roof. Finally on Sunday just before dusk, the snow stopped and the sun shone a weary, sputtery light on the horizon and the people started to come out of their houses, thickly bundled, with their shovels and their snow blowers. They waved to each other from across the cul-de-sac and called, isn't this something? But it's good exercise! And the driveways and the sidewalks were cleared and in the morning the snowplow cleared the roads and every cul-de-sac then had its own private mountain and the children climbed it and tunneled through it and slid down it and they made forts and pummeled each other with snowballs and the brilliant sun shone strong and the people marveled at the pristine beauty of it all, of white snow against a blue china sky and then come Friday the clouds rolled in, the forecasters broadly smiling said more was on the way and by Friday afternoon it was coming down hard, again, and the people shook their heads in line at the grocery store and at the liquor store and said things like, here we go again! and laughed as they walked away with bottles of wine and expensive liqueurs to warm the blood. Must stock up on essentials, they said. And by ten o'clock the Patterson's front door was completely blocked. Jenny Patterson phoned her neighbor across the cul-de-sac. Look out your window, she said. Can you believe this? They laughed and talked about what they were going to eat and drink that night, trading recipes. Saturday it was still snowing and the children who had siblings were fighting and the children without siblings were crabby from having no one to play with, so the parents bundled their children and told them to go outside, but stay close to the house. All the snowmen now had large, erect penises and rictus smiles on their faces. The snow was drifting as high as ten feet in some places and those who emerged to shovel only nodded to each other grimly through their balaclavas. Margaret Grayson was standing at her kitchen sink when she heard a muffled noise and looked out the window and saw her son Josh up to his neck in snow and screaming. She could not get the window open to yell to him but sent her older son out to rescue Josh. The older son dragged a toboggan up the snowdrift, the snow coming to above his knees, lifting a leg and plunking it down, lifting plunking doggedly as Josh continued to scream and cry. The older brother stopped and buried his hands into the snow and under Josh's armpits and pulled him straight up and out of the snowdrift. One of Josh's boots came off in the snow. The brother couldn't retrieve it. He put Josh on the toboggan and pulled him by its rope down the snowdrift and back around to the front of the house. The weather repeated itself the next weekend and the weekend after that. The parents laughed and poured amber liqueur into their snifters. Let's invite the neighbors, let's feast against the winter and so they put twelve-year-old Annelise in charge of all the kids. The neighbors came over on snowshoes with poles in their hands and their children strapped to their backs. Inside, they shed their gear and sent all the children to the basement with Annelise, who had never been in charge of anyone besides her little brother, Cal, before. All twelve children sent to the basement and the music was turned up loud and the adults did shots and cursed the snow and Bill Watley pissed out the back door, watching to see if his yellow stream would harden into ice in mid-air. It did not. The snow covered the windows and blocked the front door and the adults laughed and danced and paired off while Annelise corralled the children and the babies and the toddlers in the basement. She made them all watch *Oceans Eleven*, even the baby, propped up with pillows, and crept upstairs and stole a bottle of spiced rum and took it back down and sat in the flickering light of the big screen and took little sips every time one of the children whined and little Logan crawled on top of her when she passed out and stuck her finger in Annelise's nose and the snow continued to fall for days and they all stayed in the same house. The couples paired and re-paired and the children came up and raided the cupboards and the fridge and ate standing up, at a loss, and after a while the snowplows didn't bother to come and the newspapers stopped the presses and the mail ceased and the cold moon rose over the wide expanse of frozen, crusted snow every night until seven months later when it had finally melted off, and the light-up Christmas deer and the light-up Christmas angels emerged whole and undamaged and Josh Grayson's boot lay on the cool, frightened grass but nobody looked for it and nobody cared.

MOVEMENT

The baby cries. A fax machine starts up, humming. The man with a lopsided walk comes into the room and reads. He leans over and touches the cold window glass. The baby pulls himself to standing in his crib. The man with his head down, lopes away. The baby twists and falls on his wet bottom.

A woman calls out.

The baby pulls himself to standing in his crib. He leans over and touches the cold window glass. A man with a lopsided walk comes into the room and reads. The baby twists and falls on his wet bottom. The baby cries. The man with his head down, lopes away. A fax machine starts up, humming.

A woman lifts the baby from the crib.

A woman and a man enter the room. The baby cries lopsided. A woman starts up, pouting. The man twists and falls. The fax machine leans over, lopes away. A woman calls out. The baby with his head down, reads. The man cries, touching the glass cold window.

The man pulls himself to standing.

The lopsided baby starts up. A woman leans over, calls out. The fax machine cries. The man enters the window and touches the cold glass room. A woman with her head down, reads. The man cries. A woman pulls herself to standing. A woman twists and falls.

The baby lopes away, humming.

The baby enters the cold glass room. The lopsided man pulls himself to standing. A woman cries. The man calls out. The fax machine falls. The baby twists and falls. A woman leans over and lifts the machine from the crib. The man, loping. A woman falls. The baby falls. Humming.

SEARCHING FOR SAMUEL BECKETT

At the Cimetière Montparnasse he offers the girl his raincoat. I'm searching for Samuel Beckett, he says, and holds an umbrella over her as she consults her map. We're close, she says, pointing. I'll go with you. Then we can visit Simone de Beauvoir. My name is Scarlet. She closes her eyes. And I have been widowed twice. He thinks she looks too young for that. After, he says, we can grab a pint. The sleeves of his coat hang black and wet, to her knees. She smells like candy cigarettes. They stand in front of Beckett's grave. A three-legged cat shivers raindrops off its back. Scarlet flaps her wings and flies away.

SKINNY LULLABY AT THE LIZARD LOUNGE: SCHENECTADY

The bartender looks like Ed Sullivan. Or Richard Nixon. Shoulders to ears. Stroking his chin. "Is there any place to get chicken fried steak in this town?" We need answers and direction. Barkley says, "Meanwhile, back at the farm," narrating his own life story. Tells the bartender he looks like Boris Karloff only not as pretty and the bartender says, "I am a direct descendent of Charlemagne," to which Barkley replies, "So's my dog." Barkley says, "And the night drags on just like every other night, and the couple stumbles out into the street." We say shit and stamp our feet on the pavement, shoot breath from our nostrils like morning horses. Barkley pulls me close, whispers in my ear, "And the couple escapes to Naples, where it's not so cold." I tell him it is, it's cold as hell in Naples. Drag him back inside. The lady on the stage is skinny-singing something Joni Mitchell. We drink fuzzy navels. Get sleepy. Slide into each other like river otters.

ANOTHER STORY ABOUT ME AND SOME GUY

We met because I hate the actor Bruce Willis. I knew he was in the movie, I thought I could manage, but eventually I had to excuse myself to the lobby. That's when I saw Martin Ripley blowing out his sinuses into a napkin. I squirted butter on my popcorn and said, Is there any chance you could do that outside? He gave me a destroyed look that, I confess, broke my heart. He was super tall and slightly malformed in a way that indicated possible chromosome damage. Do you like Bruce Willis? I asked, and he said, Sure, who doesn't like Bruce Willis? And I said, Me, I can't stand him, and Martin Ripley said, Well. . . . He tossed the napkin and asked if I'd like to go with him. Where, I said, and he said, Anywhere. Jupiter. Cincinnati. He said first he had to take Maalox to his mother and there was the dry cleaning to pick up, a book to return. I thought about the guy I left in the theater, but here was Martin Ripley, smiling and introducing himself and shaking my hand. I looked up into his face, the asymmetry of his jaw like the asymmetry of my chest and I said, Let's go. Puffs of steam rose out of the asphalt and the sun on the melting snow hurt my eyes and Martin Ripley drove as if the two of us were on a long trip, something important and urgent, as if someone far away had died and here we were, speeding to the wake.

II.

They don't want to grow big and strong, they want to be left alone.

SHOEBOX

Their parents worry about them because they are so thin. Their mother fries steaks, untrimmed, in butter, mashes full cream into the potatoes. They cradle spoonfuls of food on their tongues and when their father says, "Chew that up and swallow it," they do, but the feel of it sliding down their throats is an agony.

They don't want to grow big and strong, they want to be left alone. They want to walk out to the open field behind their house, talk low, pluck caterpillars from the milkweed. Soon, there will be monarch butterflies the size of their mother's hands.

They get a hold of their aunt's cigarettes. They learned to read last year so they pass the pack back and forth, reading the warning label. They try to smoke the cigarettes, but their lungs are small and rigid, like stones in their chests. They lie down in the prairie grass and clutch each other, imagine dying together under fat clouds.

Their aunt comes to watch them sometimes when their parents have to go into Osage. As soon as the car disappears down the long, gravel driveway, she turns to them and says, "Go. Be One with Nature." The aunt drinks Seven & Sevens and sits on the screened porch, one hand squirming like a puppy under the blanket on her lap. Some smell rises up out of the aunt they can't identify. They are careful not to get too close.

In town, there is a school and there are other children. They know this because the aunt has told them. They sit on the floor in the far corner of the porch, staring at the ham salad sandwiches she made for them.

"You two fit inside a shoebox when you were born," the aunt says. "This big." She holds her hands up.

They have heard the story, how their mother swaddled them tightly together in one receiving blanket and their father put them in the box and took a picture. He sent it into the local newspaper. The photo ran on the front page. After that, their mother did not speak to their father, or anyone, for one full month.

They want to hear more about the town but are afraid to ask.

"You think I care if you eat those sandwiches? I do not. I'll stuff them down the disposal and not say a word," the aunt says.

The aunt has lupus. Her face is flat and round as a plate. A red rash sits on the bridge of her nose and across her cheeks like a pair of reading glasses. She regards the girls with her little eyes.

They read the Bible and the stories their mother types up for them. The children in the stories are forever naughty and forever in peril. In the end, the children repent and all is well. Still, God looms over their shoulders as they play, disappointed and angry.

They press their palms over a triangle of sunlight on the edge of the blanket. A truck rattles past on the road behind the stand of evergreen trees. Both girls turn their heads and listen hard.

WATERMELON

It was like the time we broke icicles dripping from the low eaves and brandished them like swords, slashing and sparkling, and you cut my cheek and dropped your weapon. Or the time we got up early and hiked until we came to a cliff and looked down into the valley covered in dew and you made to push me over the edge, but grabbed me around my waist before I fell. The night you ran away, you stood under the barn light, tapping your fist on your palm while I called you names, saying I never liked you anyway, ugliestworstmosthorrible brother ever. You left, hitchhiked all the way to Houston, and one night, months later, we looked up and saw you at the table eating watermelon in the dark.

THE HOLLOW

Afternoons, the girls play in the hollow. The heat buckles their energy and sweat drips into their eyes. Their mother works hard, but the girls are unkempt and secretive, given to a layered, sarcastic wit. Their mother bakes olive bread and cinnamon rolls. She is never cross, but occasionally she has quiet days where she doesn't speak to the girls. It is as if her head is wrapped in gauze with two holes for her eyes.

The school is two miles away and the girls walk. In this day and age! It is a matter of pride for the mother that the girls walk to school, rain or shine. "We can do anything," she tells them. "There is nothing we can't do!"

They live on the edge of town. There is a corn-field behind their house. When the wind blows, it is like the hands of many children clapping.

Their mother wears a device over her ear. It is a telephone. She walks around in public places, talk-ing and gesturing, sometimes swearing. The girls are frightened because their mother looks like a crazy person. She will look at them and say, "What? What are you staring at?"

The woman at True Value Hardware has pigtails and a hunched, contemplative posture. She asks, "What is the nature of your problem?"

The girls spin and jump. The nature of their problem! They want to take the woman in the blue apron behind the doors with the sign that says "Authorized Personnel Only" and tell her everything. That their mother sits in the garage when she gets home and leaves the car running and she cranks 101.7 The Rock and closes the garage door. The girls are young, but they are not stupid. They run down the stairs and push the garage door opener. Their mother reclines in the driver's seat. She sings along with her eyes closed. She doesn't hear the garage door open. When the song is over, she opens her eyes and is annoyed. "Why are you up? Get back to bed." But then she comes in and lets them pull off her shoes, she lets them put rainbow clips in her hair. She lets them watch *Unsolved Mysteries* until she falls asleep on the couch.

But their mother answers the woman. "My door has come off its hinges," she says and she shows her the broken hinge, the stripped screws.

The mother has started a home business, selling her goods to local grocery stores. She puts on black polyester pants, kitten heels, and a tailored blouse. She has frosted her hair. The girls do not like the way her bottom looks in the pants, like the thorax of an ant. They don't like her striped hair.

She talks to suppliers on the phone. She needs plastic bags and paper trays for the cinnamon rolls. She needs only plastic bags for the olive bread. Both require labels. The mother has designed the labels herself, working late at night on her computer. She calls her products "Goodness Gracious," which the girls think is dumb. Behind her back, they say, "Goodness gracious, this is awful!" and "Goodness gracious, I'm going to puke!"

The labels feature a smiling sun. The girls think they could draw a better one, but the mother says they don't appreciate her primitive style. The mother thinks this is hilarious. They do not want the olive bread or the cinnamon rolls. They ask for Kraft macaroni and cheese. They want Kids' Cuisine.

Their father has a new apartment he has furnished lavishly with Norwegian style furniture. The girls think it looks like a doctor's office with the magazines fanned out on the coffee table. The rooms smell like toothpaste.

He takes them to the places he used to work. He paces around outside the building. They struggle to keep up. There are windows, but they can't see inside. He turns and says, "Does anybody have to wee?"

He rushes them through the revolving door. The security guard puts up his hand. "You've been told," he says. He's a giant, taller and wider than their father.

"Hey, man, my daughters have to pee."

The security guard looks at the girls and shakes his head. "Sorry kids," he says. Their father sits outside on a cement bench, smoking, while the girls chase each other around the topiary.

He drops them home and there's soup in the crock pot, bubbling over. The floor is slick with flour. The girls sweep and wipe and eat from bowls on the back porch. They catapult navy beans into the grass. "Fine dining, fine dining!" they cry.

Later, they are woken by laughter. The girls tumble from their beds and look out the window. It is their mother, beyond the hollow on the edge of the cornfield in the blue night, her arms wild, waving down the moon.

FLORIDA

Every morning Emmeline changes out of her wet nightgown and goes into the bathroom and shakes her mother's Cashmere Bouquet talcum powder all over her body and into a fresh pair of underpants before she dresses for school. For about an hour she smells like perfume. Once, she saw her dad put Ban roll-on on his armpits and then swipe a big "X" of it across his chest. She tried this, but the kids at school said Ban roll-on smells worse than piss.

She asks her mother if she can take a bath in the mornings. "But how will you ever learn if you don't suffer the consequences?" her mother says, pointing to her chin. "You have cereal there."

"So be it," Emmeline says.

Dick Fencl draws pictures of army planes and war scenes during class. At recess, he stands inside the monkey bars and sings "The Ballad of the Green Berets." He and Emmeline are both on the chunky side. They don't climb the monkey bars and everybody leaves them alone there. Emmeline wishes Dick Fencl would sing something a little more up-tempo.

They're getting their history papers back today. They were supposed to write a biography about a person from Civil War times. She was going to write about Abraham Lincoln but then found a book about his wife, Mary Todd Lincoln.

Mary Todd Lincoln reminds her of her Aunt Janine, who takes off every few months and drives to Florida and Emmeline's mom and grandma have to track her down and commit her. When she's not being committed, though, she's okay. She paints Emmeline's toenails and gives her sips of the cocktails she learned to make tending bar at Vic's Tavern. In her paper, Emmeline compares Mary Todd Lincoln's crazy, which involved spending lots of money and going to séances, with her Aunt Janine's, which involves wearing cowgirl outfits and running with strange men.

So all the kids get their papers back except Emmeline. Sister Valeria calls her up.

"This," she says, flapping the paper on her desk, "is filth and nonsense." She's glaring at her. Behind her, Pope Paul and President Nixon are glaring at her too.

Emmeline wants to say, "So be it," but she can't open her mouth. She's sweating in her wool jumper (with the embroidered heart for the Sacred Heart of Jesus) and that stink melds with her usual pissy smell. Sister Valeria wrinkles up her nose and tears up the paper on Mary Todd Lincoln and orders her to write another one, twice as long. Emmeline is made to kneel in the back of the room and say a rosary. Out loud.

The floor hurts her knees. The kids are turning around in their seats to look at her. Dick Fencl is smiling goofily, giving her the thumbs up.

If she closes her eyes and breathes deep enough, she finds she doesn't smell so bad. *blessedisthefruitofthywooomJesus* The words make her feel like she's all alone in a shiny new place. She wonders if Dick Fencl feels like this when he's singing about the Green Berets. *nowandatthehourofourdeathamen*

Mary Todd Lincoln was holding her husband's hand when he was shot in the back of the head at Ford's Theater. After the funeral, she holed up in the White House for six weeks, and then one day she put on a fancy black dress and went to Chicago. Like that.

WREN

Her name was Renee Chu, but she was always Wren to me. My mother never let me play with her. "That child is as fragile as cracked glass," she'd say. I only really wanted to talk to her and have her talk to me. I wondered if her voice was like a bird's, soft and sweet, or if she could talk at all.

We lived across the street, kitty-cornered from Wren and her parents in one of the big, family-sized homes. There were six of us, including our parents. We were all taller than average, with long arms and legs and freckles and bushy hair. Our faces were grotesquely ruddy, our eyes bright and flashing. Every early evening, while Mother prepared dinner in big pots and cast-iron fry pans, our father had us outside on the front lawn, throwing a football or playing catch or tag. The back yard was larger and fenced, but our father liked to display us like some of the men in the neighborhood displayed their new cars.

In summer we ate at sundown, around a large table set up on the front porch. Mother would bring out salads and fried catfish and a pitcher of iced tea. We tore into our food under the ceiling fan and listened to the bug zapper fry mosquitoes and flies and moths on the other side of the screens.

We'd see Mr. and Mrs. Chu moving up the street, each holding onto one of Wren's tiny hands, their bodies curved inward on either side of her like parentheses.

One evening our mother joined in the games instead of making supper. Father grabbed her and held her tight around her waist and she struggled to free herself. My brothers and I yanked on Father's arms and legs, screeching and laughing as fireflies lifted out of the grass around our ankles.

Mother stopped struggling and Father loosened his grip and we all turned to see Wren and her parents on their nightly walk. Mother gathered us all around her, hushing us. We were panting and sweaty and unable to keep still.

Father picked up the forgotten football and smacked it against his palm. Mr. Chu nodded and Father nodded back. Wren's mother glanced at our mother. Some maternal understanding, like heat lightning, flashed in the space between them. I couldn't see Wren's eyes, but it seemed she was looking at me. I wanted to cross the street and touch her white cheek. I wanted to tell her my name.

Later Mother told us Wren was going to live in a home for sick children, but I didn't understand this. Wren was not sick, only very small.

That night I dreamed that I had hammered together a home for Wren. She would live there forever, surrounded by a thousand bright blue butterflies. And she would emerge from time to time to smile at me from behind a window of cracked glass.

AUTHENTIC SMORGASBORD DINNER

After the swim, Harold said he'd take us to the Sveden Haus for an authentic smorgasbord dinner. Our clothes stuck to our skin. He drove a converted school bus all around town. We hung our heads out the windows, like dogs. The inside of the Sveden Haus was dark and cold. Harold ordered a beer. He had a lot of beers. He said, "I'm sorry, kids. Harold has lost his balance." He had oversized lips and fingers. There was lint in the creases of his hands. His shoes were big black boxes at the end of his legs. He never took them off, even at the pool. We piled our plates with sweet pickles and fruit cocktail and meatballs and the little buns. We watched him wipe foam from his mouth. I smelled the chlorine on my arm and shivered. He said, "We'll do this another time" and I said, "But we are doing it, Harold." He didn't eat at all. He made drawings of us on the napkins, the pencil buried in his paw. Me with my two missing teeth, my brother in profile, frowning.

He talked about the war, ticking off his accomplishments. My brother said, "I can't believe they let you in." He talked to Harold the way he talked to me. Harold said, "I was okay then. I was perfect!" The waitress gave us cookies, told Harold he had nice grandchildren and Harold said thanks and winked at us. That day, Harold drove us all the way to the state border in his bus. He said he wanted to take a picture of us with one foot in Iowa and one foot in Misery. We hit a bump and flew from our seats. My brother threw up. From the rearview, Harold looked at us as if we were something brand new.

TENDERONI

My boyfriend and I grab our bikes and pedal across town for a parade that has probably been cancelled. Ahead, Mark's skinny calves pump, his Day-Glo rain poncho flaps behind him like a flag. He stops and gets off the bike and I catch up to him.

"Oh, damn," I say. "A kitty."

"It looks sort of lumpy," he says. There's a drop of rain holding on to the tip of his nose and steam rising from his shoulders. "We should move it."

There's a big to-do for several minutes as he searches for something to push it with. He tells me he doesn't want to use his bare fucking hands and I tell him of course. No one would. He finds a sodden cardboard box and peels off one side of it and shapes it into a sort of scoop.

"These ponchos are worthless."

"Stop goading me," he says. He's trying to work the cardboard under the kitten's carcass. He takes off his sneaker and nudges it. Stuff oozes out, soiling the toe of his shoe.

A car comes and we go back to the side of the road. It weaves around the kitten, but another one comes behind and roars right over it, flattening and severing its head from its body and we go back out and stare at it awhile.

"Put your shoe back on, Baby."

He studies my face and tells me that if I have to smoke, if I'm going crazy, I can go clog up my lungs under the viaduct, and I tell him I'm not going crazy yet.

The scoop falls apart in his hands. His glasses are splattered with rain. He pulls them off and rubs his bruised-looking face, the new whiskers on his chin. I hate watching him struggle but he struggles a lot so I'm getting used to it.

"Fuck," he says. "And fuck and fuck and fuck and fuck."

Under my poncho, I clench and unclench my hands. My cigarettes are in my pocket, but I leave them. "Baby, it seems like there are people whose whole job it is to remove dead animals like we have here. I feel crummy. And I have to pee. I want to take a bath and go back to bed and sleep for a hundred hours."

"I'm sorry," he says. "This is awful, isn't it?"

The wind stirs up and blows my hood back. The rain comes harder, in waves. "Only if I'm not still your baby." I swallow rain and move closer. "Only if I'm not still your tenderoni."

"Oh," he says. He pats my head and he's never patted my head before.

He stoops and picks up the kitten's smooshed head and its body and the pieces are so small in his hands. Together, we walk to the side of the road and I watch as he chucks them, hard, into a patch of high weeds.

FINE GIRL

Sue had a boyfriend who lived in a room on the East side. She wanted me to meet him. She put on her mother's bra with the lace all over it and a tight shirt and we ducked out the back door. We rented a tandem bicycle from the Sinclair station and pedaled across the Cedar River on the 4th Street Bridge a long ways past the downtown and the library and the jail and the courthouse, the old neighborhoods zooming past us like a filmstrip. Sue sat in front, steering, her hair flipping back into my mouth.

A staircase on the outside of the house led to the boyfriend's room. He came to the door in a pair of jeans and no shirt. Chest all skinny and white. Sue and I sat on his bed and he sat on a beanbag chair, chomping on an apple under a black light poster of Elton John wearing those great big shoes.

The boyfriend said he wished he could get a job at Deere and make some real money. Just give me a chance is all I ask, he said. Sue and I looked at each other. Sue'd told me he had a mustache and I guess I could see it.

I pulled off my sneaker. The boyfriend said, Gross. I have a pebble, I said, shaking it. The hair on your stomach is gross, too. It curled like a vine from his belly button down into top of his jeans.

The boyfriend was twenty years old. Sue said he might join the Army. She said he might get a car. Sometimes, she said, he called her "Baby."

The boyfriend motioned with his fingers and Sue got up and sat on his lap. I fiddled with the knob on the radio and found a station playing Brandy. I turned up the volume and closed my eyes and danced, imagining I was a fine girl.

Sue's voice came through the music. Jesus, how about some privacy, she said. The boyfriend's eyes were half-closed. The apple lay tipped on its side on the floor, turning brown.

Do you know people make dolls out of dried apples? I said. But all the dolls end up looking like old people. I was still kind of dancing.

Sue said, Are you going to cry about it?

They went back to squirming around on the beanbag chair, and I was wiping my face, thinking of night crawlers when you put them in a can of dirt.

Outside, a kid was sitting in the grass, twirling the tandem's wheels. He said, Do you need this, Lady, and I said, Yeah, but I'm a kid like you and you shouldn't call people ladies who are kids. I got on the bike and rode it back across the bridge. The back kept going its own way, tipping me over. I had to stand on the pedals to make it go.

EMPTY

It rains all over them. Their hair and their clothes droop. Their bare feet slap the pavement. Droplets cling to their noses. They don't duck and run. These kids. Even their underwear is soaked. The place reeks of manure and corn dogs and Tom Thumb donuts, wet belly buttons and Tiger Boy and diesel fuel and cows and beer. The one boy's hunched over, trying to light a cigarette, and the other says, Man, that's the saddest thing I've ever seen. And the exchange student says, Ya! The other boy lugs a large stuffed Homer Simpson whose yellow bleeds onto his shoulder. Look at us, the girl says, we're so unkempt and sorry. We need mothering.

The boys laugh, but the girl's mom said it to her all the time. She remembers her mom's bed in the dining room, under the chandelier, and, after she was gone, her dad sitting next to it, eating a tenderloin out of a white bag. I'm on empty, the girl says.

I want something good. Also, that cigarette looks like a tampon.

They'd spent all their money on the freaks and Skee-Ball and pooled their tickets for the Homer Simpson. The other boy plops him onto the plastic cow outside Estel Hall and leaves him sitting there, slightly askew. The others look at him. What? he says. He was getting heavy.

See, that shows what kind of friend you are, the one boy says. He flicks the cigarette and wipes the rain from his face. A lousy fucking friend. Inside the Exhibit Hall the 4H-ers play Crazy Eights and Snap. They're sitting on their coolers full of pop and candy bars and sandwiches. They tip back their caps and laugh. Fans blow, and the animals sprawl and blink and fart expansively.

The girl says, I'm cold, let's go in there, but the boys don't listen, except the exchange student, who says, Ya! She stands on tiptoes, holding his cow-like head in her hands. Let's go in one of the shops and take something. You could get away with it, you're a foreigner. (They all want a dog. The one boy has a cat, but he wants a dog. The girl wants a dog you can carry in your purse, and the other boy wants a real dog and he wants the dog to have balls. If they had a dog they wouldn't be here. They'd be some-place better. With their dogs. The exchange student looks at their faces and nods. Dogs!)

III.
It's as if there are little men inside her head, wielding hammers.

NIGHT AT THE RESERVOIR ON AIRLINE DRIVE

My brother's friend, Del, said, hey little girl, wanna Tootsie Roll? I asked him if there was anything he could do to make my Slurpee taste better and he poured a healthy dose of vodka in. That summer it was vodka slurpees, vodka Mountain Dews, vodka lemonades. Dad had gotten custody of us, which meant we were pretty much left to our own devices. Del and I watched my brother toe his way to the edge of the cottonwood branch that arched over the reservoir. My brother, meaning to dive, and Del questioning the depth of the water. It had been quite bright with the moon but now thunderclouds roiled and gyred above us and my brother was something you could only see if you didn't look directly at him. I was 14 but could pass for 16 if I wore makeup, which I did. That night, I'd decided if Del put his tongue in my mouth, I'd let him. Far off, we saw a lightning strike and Del yelled up, you still there buddy? We thought maybe he'd changed his mind, was coming back down, when we saw his baseball cap copter to the ground. You don't want to get that wet, Del laughed and picked it up, put it on his own prematurely balding head. A car pulled up and a bunch of boys tumbled out, staggered to where we were. I was wearing my honeydew colored bikini but that night it looked gray like everything else. You could only really see white teeth, bluish arms and legs. My brother called, who's there? They were boys he knew, older boys, who yelled jump, jump you sonofabitch. I remember the crack of the branch and Del, dragging him out of the water, pounding him on the chest, and then the ambulance. I remember how relieved we were, later, to hear it was only a concussion and Del had been crazily, comically trying to administer CPR to a boy who didn't need it. And my brother lying on the couch for days, how he became now, not even sullen, just a quiet fellow who liked to stay inside, who sometimes stared at his hands and asked why'd it hurt so much?

RODNEY AND CHELSEA

1. Tangerines

Rodney and Chelsea have decided this is the day. They are sixteen years old and they are in love. Neither of them has ever done it, though Rodney has come close with a girl he worked with at Dairy Queen who smelled like French fries and who had perfect, melon-sized breasts. Chelsea's breasts are more the size of tangerines, but he likes them. He likes that she smells like Fruit Loops and that her front teeth overlap slightly. Her mouth is glossed. He slips his tongue inside.

2. Bear Spirit

"Rodney's an old man's name," Chelsea's mom says and calls him Rascal instead. It makes Rodney feel like a Labrador.

Chelsea's mom believes that life is a celebration and that people should live in the Now. Chelsea has an older brother named Royal. Nobody knows where the hell he is. He ran away from the halfway house downtown, the place Chelsea's mom said was his best chance and hope. He has a behavior disorder which involves beating people up. He doesn't know his own strength is what Chelsea's mom says. He has a bear spirit. He is unruinable.

The last guy he beat up now walks with a cane.

3. The Bunnies

Chelsea's father left when Royal was ten and Chelsea was a newborn. Every Easter, he sends Chelsea a six-foot Easter bunny and now she has sixteen huge Easter bunnies and there are no more places to sit in Chelsea's house. Sometimes people sit on the bunnies' laps or sometimes they just stand, looking around or sometimes they sit on the floor.

4. A Small Complication

Their first date, Rodney plucked a daffodil from Chelsea's garden and presented it to her at the door. And Chelsea's mom gave them Boone's Farm, mixed with a splash of 7UP. All three of them got a little drunk, sitting on the porch watching the sun go down and a full moon rise. Chelsea's mom insisted on driving Rodney home. Before he got out of the car, she pulled his face to hers and kissed him, hard.

5. About Rodney's Parents . . .

Rodney doesn't have any siblings. He feels lucky, given the circumstances. His mother died of cancer when he was five. He remembers standing on tiptoe to reach a cookie off a plate on the counter and her hand slapping his away. He tries to really see that hand, to see something about it that is especially hers, but it always ends up being just a hand.

Rodney's father is a podiatrist who is working on his overall fitness. Every day at dawn, he walks the perimeter of the cul-de-sac, gripping fifty-pound dumbbells in each hand. In warm weather he goes without a shirt, his burgeoning muscles gleaming. He makes three trips around, bobs his chin to Chelsea's mom who watches from her kitchen window, and lays the dumbbells on the porch in the special box. He consumes nothing but protein: lamb chops, sausages, steaks as thick as two hands clamped together. He will never love another woman, he promises Rodney, who really doesn't care if he does or not. Rodney only wants his father to be happy, which his father assures him he is.

6. Clinical

Two bunnies sit in opposite corners of Chelsea's bedroom. One is missing an eye and one's polka-dotted ear is nearly torn off. Rodney and Chelsea undress in a clinical manner and fold their clothes as if, together, they have decided to join the Army. Rodney has seen parts of Chelsea but never the whole and now he stands before her and reaches out to touch one tangerine. Unsure of what to do with her own hands, Chelsea simply places them on Rodney's shoulders.

She's afraid to get closer because his thing is standing up. She digs her toes into the pink shag rug and closes her eyes. The breeze through the window is making the shutters flap against the window frame and Rodney's breath smells like oatmeal and grape jelly.

7. The Now

At this moment Chelsea's dad is getting fired from his job selling tires in Terre Haute and her mom is hunched over a patient, scraping plaque in an office downtown, thinking of that kiss, and Royal's getting the shit kicked out of him in a bar in Tucson. At this moment, Rodney's dad's outside on the curb, sweating, coughing, turning blue, as Rodney kisses Chelsea. Like howling into her mouth.

MORO

My parents said it was unbecoming for a young girl to wear eye shadow, especially eye shadow that sparkled when I closed my eyes. The shade was called "Morning Sky." The case had a spring-loaded hinge so, after checking myself in the tiny mirror, I could snap it shut with a delicate pinch of just two fingers.

I've learned it's easy to startle a newborn with a sudden noise. It throws its arms out and its head back. This is called the "Moro Reflex." The first time Henry did this I thought he was dying. I rushed over and pinned his hands down to the bed and planted my mouth over his and when he started to cry I rolled over beside him and started crying too.

When my friend Melanie's baby was stillborn, she and her mother were given one hour to take photos if they wanted to. They called me and asked me to bring my new digital camera. When I arrived, I had spots of milk on my blouse so I kept my coat on. I hoped they couldn't smell it. Melanie's mom was sliding lipstick over Melanie's mouth the way little girls put makeup on a doll. I didn't realize at first the lump on the hospital bed was Melanie's baby.

"That's Cory," Melanie said and her mother threw her hands up. "You made me smear it!"

I brought along the "Morning Sky" eye shadow and Henry's satin baptismal gown. Melanie's mother thanked me for the eye shadow and dusted it over Melanie's eyelids like she was waving a magic wand. My parents would've said they both looked like tarts, but I thought they looked nice. I held up the gown, but Melanie shook her head.

"Let's just take the picture," she said. I settled the bundle on her lap, and moved her arms to cradle it. Melanie looked at me and said, "Thanks for not bringing Henry," and I thought, of course I wouldn't bring him.

I raised the camera and backed up a couple of steps. Melanie's mother smiled until she remembered and her lips turned down. "I guess we won't be going to The North Pole," Melanie said. That was our plan, to take our babies to the North Pole in Colorado Springs to have their photos taken with Santa.

I snapped the picture, then showed it to Melanie and her mom. Melanie lifted her hand to touch the camera and the baby slid sideways down her lap. "That turned out pretty good," she said and I touched my friend's hair where it had been carefully combed and parted to one side, but I can't remember what I said.

MAIDENHEAD TO OXFORD

I stand hugging my light sweater around me on Platform 6 at Maidenhead Station. On the opposite side of the rails, men in dark suits and women in crisp blouses and skirts move up the stairs in waves and spill onto Platform 4 to await the train to Paddington.

On this side of the rails there are only the four of us: the old couple sitting on one of the curving, wrought iron benches, the tall man, and me. A gust of wind releases fat drops of rain and the commuters on the other side draw back in unison.

I settle myself on a bench and look at the clock. The train isn't due for another five minutes. I hear a faraway rumble that becomes a roar and look up to see the train to Paddington.

It pauses to eat up the dark suits and the crisp blouses and skirts. The cars pull away, revealing a handful of commuters who had presumably rushed up the stairs to closing doors, and who now watched the departing train with resignation before slumping back under cover to flick open their newspapers. When I look up again, six minutes have passed and the rain is falling steady and silent. I blow into my cupped hands.

The tall man has not left his spot on the edge of the platform.

A chime sounds and an announcement that sounds like a recording tells us that the 9:15 to Oxford has been "regrettably delayed." The old couple grouse briefly, then turn their attention back to their guidebooks.

The tall man stands with his long arms hanging straight down as if they're paralyzed. He is soaked through now, his brown and gray hair flat to his skull, his face like his sweater, drooping. I want to go to him, pull him under the shelter like one would do to a small child.

I decide to call him Ralph.

The single headlight of the train shines dimly through the gray rain. The old couple rises. The platform shudders as the train approaches and slows to a stop. Another gentle chime, this time from the train itself, and the doors whoosh open. Ralph steps in and I follow behind him into the warmth and light of the car.

He has chosen a seat farther down the aisle. Within minutes downtown Maidenhead gives way to the countryside and the meandering Thames on my right.

I get a cup of tea in the club car and carry it back to my seat. Sunlight breaks through the clouds and shines through the window directly on the back of Ralph's head, creating from his bald spot a halo.

The river widens and narrows as we move along. At times I can't see it at all. At Didcot Parkway, Ralph suddenly rises and exits the train. I watch him step onto the platform, looking around as if he's not quite sure what to do next.

I gather up my bag. My lipstick and pen spill out, but I leave them.

Just as I get up I see a woman approach him. She has long, blonde hair that blows behind her in ropes. She raises her arms to embrace him. He sinks into her.

The chime sounds and I fall back into my seat. The train lurches then accelerates out of the station. The old man is asking me a question. I turn in my seat to watch Ralph and the woman on the platform. They stand holding each other for as long as I can see them. Probably longer.

ORLANDO

Lori likes the man who sits at the hotel bar every other Friday night and gives her tissues when she starts to cry. Lori would like not to cry so much and she's not even sure why she cries, but if the man is there, in his rumpled suit and scuffed shoes, he gives her a mournful, commiserating look and produces the tissue. He says, "It's not so bad." She can hardly hear him over the thunking music and the Happy Hour crowd, but it's what he always says, so she nods and smiles and pats his arm.

She likes that he doesn't judge, like the manager, Ike, or the other waitresses and customers. Ike told her he may have to let her go if she can't pull it together. People come here for the happiness. But when the place is overrun with customers and not enough staff, it's Ike who hides in the cooler amongst the boxes of frozen onion and calamari rings until the crisis passes or he runs out of oxygen.

Lori is too wiped out after her shift to want to do much sexually with her boyfriend, Freddie. They're like roommates now, going over the bills together in the kitchen on Sunday afternoons, walking up and down the grocery aisles afterwards, with an envelope of cash marked FOOD. Lori spends too freely. They use the envelopes so she can't go over budget. If they run out of bananas and the envelope's empty, then sorry. No more bananas.

The man at the bar says he works for a company that manufactures industrial laminates. Lori has no idea what these are, but she says, "Cool" anyway. He gives her his business card. It says, "M. Shipley, Regional Sales Representative" and when she asks, he won't say what the M. stands for, so she just calls him M. She slips him an extra Heineken sometimes, when Ike isn't watching.

Tonight, when the man hands over the tissue he asks Lori up to his room. He tells her he only wants to put his arms around her. Every time he sees her, he says, he longs to put his arms around her.

Lori finishes her shift, counts and shares her tips, unties her apron, and meets the man outside the bar. She wishes she didn't smell so much like hamburgers. The hotel's ballroom is as big as a hangar and they have to cross it to get to the elevators. One hotel employee moves from table to table with a cart, clearing up. "Hey," Lori says, and the boy says

"Hey, Lori," drawing out the vowels, but he doesn't look up.

"It looked so pretty in here earlier," she tells the man, her voice echoing. The lights had been turned down low and candlelight pinged the crystal chandeliers. Men and women in evening dress danced around the room. Now, in the bright light, the ballroom looks hung over. "I hate this shabbiness," she says.

"Please don't cry again," he says. "I'm out of tissues."

They stand at the door of his room while he fumbles for his key. Lori sniffs. "I think this is just allergies."

He takes all the cards out of his wallet and fans them, like a poker hand.

"I must have lost it," he says.

"This is a fork in the road. You can't find that key because we're not meant to go in there," Lori says, pushing up her glasses. "Also, my ears are popping. Maybe that means something."

"No, I've got it," he says. He tucks his wallet into his pocket and grabs hold of her, squeezing her. Lori lets out a little gasp. He runs his hand through her hair.

Inside, he grips a corner of the bedspread and pulls. It slides off, stiff and shiny with the residue of sex. "These never get washed," he says. "I saw a news segment where the reporter put a square of hotel room bedspread under a microscope. It looked like an ocean full of confused protozoa."

"People don't want to mess up the sheets they're going to sleep on later," Lori says. She is aware of the note of authority in her voice. She runs her hand down the front of her uniform, as if to smooth out wrinkles, and removes her shoes.

"I'm anything but fussy," the man says, kicking the bedspread into the corner.

"Oh I almost forgot," Lori pulls something wrapped in a napkin out of her purse and hands it to him.

He sets it on the dais and opens it up. "Oh. It's a sandwich."

"Do you like sandwiches?"

"Sure I do," he says.

Lori takes off her glasses and sets them on the nightstand. Without them, the furniture in the room resembles a family of amiable bears. She switches off the lamp. The man pulls her close and sighs into the back of her neck. It makes her want him.

"The maids have a break room that management doesn't even know about," Lori says. "One of the guest rooms that are supposed to be redecorated? But it's like they've forgotten about it. They have a riot in there. Parties galore. Sometimes they invite me and that means something, because I'm not the most fun person in the world."

"Could you turn around?" he says. "I want to see your face."

"The maids are crazy. This *place* is crazy. People have no idea. You know that guy we saw cleaning up? His name is Spencer. He can *dance*."

The man says, "Please turn around so I can see you."

She runs her hand up and down his arm, but doesn't move. "But this is nice," she says. "Isn't it?"

She feels his mouth on her skin, kissing, biting a little. She turns to face him and they kiss, long and slow. It is beyond her now, and the man's hands are all over her, touching her hair, her face, her body. He kisses her throat, nibbles her jaw.

Lori has a vague sense of Freddie, back at the apartment, craning his neck out the fire escape, calling for her, as if she were a lost cat. She waves her hands around as the man kisses her like she's trying to catch hold of something.

He stops and looks at her. "Are you okay?"

"We should stop," she says.

"Are you sure?"

No she is not.

The air conditioning clicks on and hums. The drapes flutter, letting in a hard line of light from the parking lot.

"Come on. Let me show you around this place," Lori says.

On the hotel roof, they can see all of Orlando, hyper and blinking and spread out for miles. The air is cool and fragrant of magnolias. Lori sits on one of the lawn chairs and pulls off her shoes.

"Don't look," she says, scrunching and splaying her toes.

"This is great," the man says, sitting next to her.

Lori's not used to being with him with so much quiet around. His voice isn't jumbled in with the bar noise, the customer noise, the music. She doesn't have to lean in and go "pardon?" when he talks to her.

Cars pass on the street below, the flags on top of the hotel across the street flutter and snap. There are a million stars, but over the city lights, the sky is a dull gray blanket. Lori remembers the night she and Freddie drove out to the country and lay flat on their backs in some farmer's field to watch a meteor shower. She said to him, "This is the most wondrous place I've ever been to." The next day, they drove by and saw the rusted cars near the farmhouse, the scum on the pond, a three-legged cat hopping among the weeds.

She walks a slow, wide circle around the man. "You're probably tired. I'm keeping you up."

"No, please. I don't want to go back to my room yet."

Lori shows him places in the hotel other people don't get to see, the kitchen, the break room. In the hotel laundry, Lori says to the two women folding a mountain of white towels, "This is my friend. His name is M." They look up and smile. Lori and the man hold hands lightly, sometimes swinging their arms as they wander around. She notices the hems of his trousers are frayed. One shoe is untied.

They pass through the ballroom again.

"I'm sorry. I can't turn on the lights. We have to be a little sneaky." Lori's focused on the exit sign, pulling on the man's hand.

She pushes open the door and they stand outside it, squinting, regarding each other. The place is deserted except for one of the housekeeping staff pushing a vacuum sweeper around the lobby. Lori picks a small camera up off the floor.

"Does it have a timer? Let's take a picture of us," the man says.

Lori laughs. "On someone *else's* camera?"

"Sure. And then we'll be good scouts and turn it in at the front desk."

He sets the timer and walks across the lobby and places the camera on the front desk. The housekeeper looks up from her vacuuming. He waves Lori over and they stand together, one-half inch apart, in front of a potted fig tree with tiny white lights woven through its branches. At the last second, the man lifts his arm to put it around Lori's shoulder, knocking her glasses askew.

She looks at him. "M., let's go back."

In bed, he kisses the top of her head and pulls her close. Lori whispers into his chest, but teenagers are tromping down the hall outside, laughing. He doesn't hear her. She's aware of her waitress uniform, twisted around her, her hair in tangles.

The man is quiet for a long while, then he starts to tell her things, about how long he has worked for the laminate company and the schedule of cities he travels to. New York, Washington, Orlando, and back. How he hates all the airports and the taxi cabs and the hotel rooms, but that is his job. He tells her that his oldest daughter has bulimia, but she's such a sweet girl, and that last year his wife found a lump. She's cancer-free now, but they don't touch anymore and they never kiss and it's kissing that he misses more than anything. He talks and Lori listens, blinking in the dark. And every now and then, he asks her if she's okay and she says she is.

A week later, as M. rides the airport shuttle to La Guardia and Lori ponders the unit price on a pound of macaroni, a couple from Ohio downloads their vacation photos onto their computer. They click through several photos of their two children,

Sy and Mandy, hugging Mickey, hugging Minnie, shaking hands with Goofy, when they come to an odd photo of a tall stranger in a wrinkled suit, with his tie undone, who is turned facing a small woman wearing crooked glasses and the kind of smile a woman wears when she's on the verge of tears.

CURE

The girl pretends she's already in New York. The thought gives her a shimmery, golden feeling behind her collarbone. Lately, everything and everyone injures her. She's become lugubrious and she's only twenty-two. She has gained the approval of the landlady who takes note of her freshly pressed uniform. It is the way I am, too, says the landlady. As if that's reason enough. The landlady, at least, will be sorry to see her go.

The customers are demanding. One man writes "Poor Service, Very Disappointing" on the back of his receipt, and the manager pins it on the bulletin board in the kitchen. The manager's a slow, peevish man with a patch of white hair on the back of his head. I am tired, she signs, for she's mute, but not deaf mute. She will work at The Filling Station for six months, saving until she has enough for a plane ticket and one-month's deposit.

The boyfriend handles rattlesnakes. It's his religion to handle rattlesnakes. Or maybe there's more to it than that. The girl doesn't believe in God, but she likes the baleful gaze of the snakes, their smooth skin. The boyfriend doesn't want her to move. He thinks she bamboozled him into loving her.

The rattlesnakes are brought to the church in a sort of carrier. The church is located in a strip mall and is only a church by reason of being a gathering place of the faithful and not by reason of being a structure like a church at all. In fact, it used to be a realtor's office. One of the church men tells the girl he likes the cut of her jib. It sounds kind of dirty. The cut of her jib.

The landlady hauls up an old typewriter and watches as the girl works on her resume. Instead of Cedar Falls, her place of birth, the girl types Cheddar Falls, but she doesn't notice. What she does notice is the way the floor rises, then falls, under her feet when she gets up to make tea, as if she were walking on an under-inflated balloon.

She starts falling down—at work, on the street, in the shower—and wonders, what now?

It's as if there are little men inside her head, wielding hammers. The people from the church say they can deliver her from her affliction. They all but guarantee it. They make her lie still on a fold-up buffet table in the church basement. It alarms her to realize that she once ate ham and beans at this table. They dance around and chant with the snakes on their shoulders. She closes her eyes and waits, but her skull bulges with pressure. She raises her hand and the people halt in contorted positions like freeze tag.

She'll go to New York anyway, on a gurney if she has to and tell the boyfriend he will live to love and fuck somebody else. No problemo, I appreciate the effort, she gestures to the church people, knowing not everyone understands sign language. In fact, hardly anyone does.

LENS

Prue was a scarecrow of a woman, thin and hard with a straight mouth. But she knew the secret for growing tulips. Her tulips were bright yellow and blood-red, eighteen inches tall in full bloom. Their heads swung round in the Kansas breeze. She worked for the county and lived alone.

A photographer came from the Wichita Eagle.

"Well, there they are," she said, pointing.

He laughed. "No, I want you, too." He made her lie flat on her stomach in the grass, her face level with the blooms. "They're exquisite," he said. "How do you do it?"

"Do you know," she said, "that strangers come round to see my flowers? Little girls in Easter bonnets trample my garden. They pick my flowers and don't ask permission."

His elbows planted in the dirt, he aimed the camera and adjusted the lens, took pictures until the sun sank low.

They entered her house through the kitchen door. The photographer unbuttoned her long cotton shirt, pulled down her loose pants. He touched her grim mouth with the tips of his fingers, ran his hands down her slim, hard body. In bed, she was silent when the photographer cried out.

Night fell and the photographer slept, one hand between Prue's legs. She lay awake and watched the light from passing cars travel the walls of her bedroom, then disappear.

MOTH WOMAN

The woman who came to pick up the bags of clothes seemed like she wanted more than clothes from us. That was what I told Greg later, that she had hungry eyes and that made him laugh. But she did have hungry eyes and long hair the color of whiskey and a way of touching her face when she talked. And Greg asked later, Why'd we let her in? She came in a beat-up Datsun. She probably took those clothes for herself. Why'd we let her in? And I reminded him that we got to talking about the moths in the basement and the woman wanted to see.

So we took her down and there they were, hundreds of them, bright green, fluttering around. Greg had thought if we turned out the light and left the sliding door open they would simply fly away, but they stayed. I sat on the top step and watched the woman go down and stand in the middle of the room, raising her hands as if to touch them, and I half expected the moths to lift the ends of her hair, the hem of her skirt, and fly away with her.

These are Luna Moths, the woman said. Do you have a walnut tree? And we said, Yeah, out there, pointing to the back yard. She said, They're mating, they'll mate all night long. Greg wanted to know what then and the woman said, They rest. How do we get them out of here, I asked and the woman said, Oh, they'll just die. They only live a week. Their journey is a short one. I stood and said, I'll go and get those bags, but it seemed like she'd forgotten all about them.

One of the moths flew directly into Greg's face and he batted at it, saying, Shit. Shit. The woman put her finger to her lips, shushing him, like, Oh no, don't swear in front of the pretty bugs, and we got pissed all over again remembering it later, like how dare she. She said, Words get embedded in a place, they settle into the walls and furniture like ghosts, to which Greg said, Horse shit, and the woman said, Are you afraid of strange ideas, and Greg said, No, I'm afraid of strange people, and we smirked at each other then because we seriously wanted this Moth Woman out of our basement. Finally she put her arms down and came upstairs and carted away the bags of clothes in her crappy little car.

The next morning I went down to the basement, and just as the woman had said, the moths had all died. At first I thought everything, the floor, the furniture, the shelves, was covered in thick, green leaves. Then I realized.

IV.
In an infinite universe
all things are
mathematically possible.

LIP

Tom Brace stands naked in front of a mirror doing something resembling the Twist. He watches his paralyzed left arm arc across his body, then swivel around and disappear behind his back. He does this over and over again. He's very high and it makes him laugh.

He's alone in his motel room, casting glances at the cable rerun of *Get Smart*, and laughing at that, too.

"I'm a parlor trick now," he says to his reflection. "A parlor trick that needs to diet." He sighs.

The Cone of Silence descends upon Maxwell Smart and his boss, that bald guy.

Last night Tom'd been beaten up by a guy with pointy teeth. He yanked Tom's arm high up behind his back. Luckily, the arm had two years before been paralyzed by a stroke, so he felt no pain, only a strange airy feeling when the shoulder joint had been forced out of its socket, as if a hole had been drilled through his skin.

"You have dust on your shoes," he said to his attacker before passing out.

Now his shoulder hangs halfway down his ribcage. He swigs some wine. "Fruit of the vine and work of human hands," he says, archly.

When he was ten, he'd fished for crappie in the Shell Rock River with his father. His father taught him how to cast his line and crank it back in slowly. He caught five, learning to render them motionless by grasping and lifting them up by the lower lip. His father told him he was a natural and took him out for pancakes so big they drooped over the sides of the plate.

Tom leans into the mirror and points to himself. "Not once did he have to tell me to watch my mouth."

Tom applies eyeliner with his working hand. He wants to look like Agent 99. He thinks about the Venus de Milo, how perfectly presented she is in the Louvre. He's going for an Agent 99 version of that.

The room's dark except for the sunset coming in where the drapes fail to meet the windowsill, and it's silent except for Maxwell Smart and his boss shouting at each other under the Cone of Silence. Tom's legs buckle, but he locks his knees and stands tall. Tonight, he will be magnificent. He will pretend he has no arms at all.

BABY, BABY

Everyone's in a hurry. Especially the men, who run for the trains and sacrifice their briefcases to the doors. Men in seats, reading newspapers or paperbacks. Ling is weary of these men. She wants to stick her pregnant belly into their noses. She looks at herself in the window. She's wearing a herringbone maternity suit with a large red bow at her neck. She looks angry and fat, but festive.

Six weeks after giving birth, Ling goes back to work downtown. She pumps her breasts in the ladies room, sitting on the toilet. Co-workers come in to pee or brush their teeth and the pump squeaks and from the stall, Ling says, sorry. . . . I'm sorry.

Before dawn, she buckles the baby into the Escort and sticks a bottle in its mouth. She leaves the car seat at the babysitter's for her husband, who collects the baby when he gets off work and drives the baby home in his Toyota. The baby listens to Bruce Springsteen in the Toyota and Moonlight Sonata in the Escort.

Ling hands the babysitter a half-cup of frozen blue milk in a baggy. The babysitter shrugs. I'll mix it with her formula, she says. You have a run in your stocking.

Ling doesn't sleep and becomes ineffectual in her job. She'd quit, but they are sort of broke. Suddenly, she doesn't know what any of it means. What does it mean? She asks her co-workers. What are the codes? What are the procedures? She types a row of question marks, eats prodigiously from a bag on her desk. Sometimes she closes her eyes and dreams that the baby has been put back into her stomach. Only now, the baby is a monkey.

On weekends, she takes the baby for long strolls. Once they'd gone as far as three miles and the baby got hungry and Ling had forgotten to pack a bottle. She ran all the way back, bumping over cracks in the sidewalk as the baby screamed.

The husband arranges for a babysitter so they can go to a Christmas party. The party is a Vegas night and they gamble at tables and make small talk with the husband's co-workers and their spouses. At the craps table, Ling whispers to the older woman next to her, I have a three month old. I can't believe I'm here. The woman offers a sip of her screwdriver.

Each working day at dusk, Ling runs into the house and kicks off her sneakers. She reaches up into her skirt and rolls down the band of her panty hose and takes the baby from her husband's lap. She lies on her back, holding the baby overhead and flies the baby back and forth in her upstretched arms. She sings: *flying all over the world looking for toys and candy* and the baby smiles and the husband laughs. And the baby's cheeks droop like water balloons. And the baby drops drool on Ling's forehead.

THIS IS DWIGHT

Ron and Bethal arrive with their son. Ron hands me a gift: two beeswax candles tied with a bow that looks like straw.

"This is Dwight."

I shake the boy's hand. "Is that you I've heard whistling in the mornings? You're a champion."

Bethal looks around. "It's roomy. I've never been inside this place."

I've invited them for nachos and margaritas. I invited everyone on the street, but they were the only ones who could make it. I am by God never moving again.

"I've made limeade for you," I tell Dwight. "You can have it in one of my margarita glasses. See, the stems are shaped like cacti."

"Oh the kitchen is tiny though," Bethal says. She takes a seat at the counter. I still have boxes everywhere.

"Dwight is always cheerful," says Ron. "Whistle

something for us, buddy."

"Wait a sec." I give the margaritas another zip in the blender and pour one out for each of us.

Dwight takes a sip of his limeade and sets down his glass. His father and mother are looking at him. His eyes are cast down, as if he's composing himself. I start to say he doesn't have to if he doesn't want to, but Bethal says, "Shh."

Dwight lifts his head and stares straight ahead and whistles "Red River Valley." When he finishes Ron and Bethal clap, so I clap too.

"Wow. That was so sad sounding. So melodious. Is that the word?"

Bethal sips her margarita. "Dwight attends a Steiner school. The children are not taught to read until they have lost all their milk teeth."

"Bravo," I say. "My mother says I didn't learn to tie my shoes until I was nine. And look at me now!"

I carry the plate of nachos out onto the deck. The three of them follow me. I want to tell them I have a little boy too and that he may come to visit sometimes, but I don't want to jinx it.

"It's a good neighborhood," Ron says, looking around. "Everyone's clean and quiet, but friendly."

"They're only friendly when they need you. You'll see." Bethal raises her glass as if she's made a toast.

"Really now. Bethal sometimes makes her points too strenuously. It's because she's so passionate."

"Well, no. That's not it," she says. Bethal's eyelids droop, like clay that's softened. I want to put my thumbs on them and push up. I hope my face doesn't look as sad as hers.

"What grade are you in, Dwight? Do you play soccer?" I top off Ron and Bethal's drinks and my own. "Seems like all the kids play soccer these days."

"Dwight made those candles we gave you," Ron says. "Didn't you, buddy?"

"But I want to hear about you," Bethal says. "Where are you from? I can't place your accent."

"I'm from Nebraska. Nebraskans have an unplaceable accent. It's like—everything and nothing at the same time."

Ron laughs. "That's marvelous!" He scoops up a nacho and pops it into his mouth.

"I've lived lots of places though."

Bethal takes Ron's hand and squeezes it. I wait for them to ask me about the places I have lived, but they don't.

Dwight has jumped up onto the deck railing. His legs are white and hairless. His tee shirt says, "Number One Rocker." It appears to have been pressed. I smell barbecue, hear people laughing.

"Well," Bethal says and she and Ron stand up.

"You don't have to leave."

Then Dwight starts to tell me about his new travel pillow. He got it at a camping supply store and it can be stuffed into a pouch no bigger than a field mouse.

"Did you know a pillow is the single most important item to ensure a traveler's comfort?" Dwight asks. Bethal says, "Shh," but I tell her no, let him talk. I like the sound of his voice.

BREATHLESS

The teacher calls. I'm slicing radishes. She doesn't want to interfere, but I should encourage Marta to make more friends. Three times I say, "I recognize the problem." I worry I may have been rude.

We have moved into this small rental because we are poor. I decorate it in bright colors and wild patterns to cheer us, but we're in mourning. My daughters' father, Rob, died of lung cancer last spring.

I buy a Valentine for my oldest child who is away at college. And Lindt truffles in a gold bag. I send them to Chapel Hill with "I love you, Lynn" written on the envelope.

Lately I dream I'm riding a bicycle at night, the moon and the stars shining on my back.

We adopt a puppy and name him Bud. We walk him under clouds the color of pencil lead. Bud is picky. He chooses his own path. I think Marta is starting to laugh again.

I bring photos of the girls to Rob's family. His mother gives me peach pie. They look at me with disdain, but I am not asked to leave.

Before Rob got sick, a former classmate shot himself. We attended the wake. The mourners were cordoned in a looping line, like Disneyland. Rob made a joke about selling tickets.

I find Marta in the closet, cutting up one of Rob's old T-shirts. We could make something out of the pieces, I suggest, stupidly. Later, Lynn calls, breathless, reading Flannery O'Connor. I tell her about Marta and she goes quiet.

We take Bud for a walk at dusk. Marta's coat is too big for her and her boots are unzipped and flopping. She turns to say something. The hood covers half her face, but I see it. Marta's face is careworn.

I'll take Marta and move back to Ohio, closer to my family. Lynn can join us when school's out. I'll get a better job and we'll buy a house there. Something modest, but comfortable. In summer we'll buy fresh strawberries and we'll eat them on the roof, under the draping branches of some enormous tree.

SPACE MAN

His girlfriend's probably surfing somewhere in California right now. She is an astrophysicist and a veteran and a triathlete, but she's never been up in space, like he is now, in a failing spacecraft. He knows it's failing by the way the engine sounds, like a tennis shoe in a dryer, and also, by the way it's spiraling out of control. Alone and aloud, Space Man employs the imperative: Eject! Eject! And girding himself for the unknown, he presses the button. Untethered, he waves to his ship as it cartwheels through space. As he, himself, cartwheels through space. He squinches his eyes shut. Jane would tell him not to be afraid, that this is an infinite universe and in an infinite universe all things are mathematically possible, even certain. And so he imagines his pretty girl, walking toward him on a boardwalk or even on Pluto or some star, a surfboard under her arm, saying see, Space Man? See?

SWICKS RULE!

My twin cousins, Margie and Mae, are manning the grill, telling me about their diverticulitis. They shake their heads. No nuts, no seeds. Their sweet hound dog, Steve, lies at our feet smelling oddly of deviled eggs and Crazy Glue.

"Steve. How's about a nice shower, boy?" I unroll the hose on the side of the twins' house and turn on the faucet. The water gurgles and whooshes its way through the coiled hose. It's brown at first, like the grass. Steve comes loping over and flops on his fat back. I spray his belly and dribble a little into his open mouth. His eyes are closed and he's wiggling from side to side, tongue hanging out, lapping the water.

"He doesn't like that," Margie says.

The twins don't match. Margie is much grayer and stouter and Mae is as tall as me and she has a terrible, unfortunate stutter. She smiles a lot.

It's the Swick Family Reunion 2008. My first family function without my wife, Lorraine. My nieces and nephews painted the banner that's taped to the garage door, with everyone's handprints, even the adults'. I have promised that later I'll give them all rides on my back, but they're a year bigger and I'm a year fatter.

A little blonde is tugging at my belt loop. "Did you bring the jigglers?" she asks and I realize to my horror that I can't think of her name. There are so many of them.

"No, Sweet Pea. I'm sorry." Lorraine used to bring those every year. The gelatin snacks shaped like, I guess, animals.

Steve wanders away and I go sit at the picnic table next to Gigi Gran and my brother, Lou. Gigi Gran is telling him how she doesn't believe in global warming, pulling her cardigan tighter around her bony shoulders.

"Pah!" she says. "And pah again!" She's never learned to modulate her voice.

"Meanwhile the narwhals are disappearing from our earth," Lou says. Lou's got his binder, the one that says "Save the Turtles" on the front. It's full of articles he's cut out and hole punched. He was captain of the debate team in high school and knows to carry his evidence around with him, just in case.

Gigi Gran leans into him and says, "Eh?" and he says, "Narwhals. Narwhals!" She waves her hand around, says, "Pah!" and starts digging invisible things out of the potato salad with her bare hands.

"Hey, I was going to eat some of that," I say.

"Oh, hello, Bob," Lou says, and then we just look at each other. Everybody's feeling awkward around me today. I want to tell them it's all right, that I'm all right, but I don't want to see their eyes when I say it.

Gigi Gran has eased her lumpy feet out of her house slippers, so I reach down and grab one and chuck it to Steve while she's not looking. He paws it to his mouth and chews on it, dolefully. The burgers smell so good and I find my stomach growling again. There's not enough food in the world for me these days. I buy Lean Cuisines and eat four of them in one sitting. All my dishes have dust on them.

"Soup's on," Margie says, bearing a huge platter of grilled burgers and hot dogs and brats.

"Thank god." I'm embarrassed to realize I said it out loud.

The twins' neighbor has shown up, uninvited, and is playing the bongos while the nieces and nephews jerk their skinny bodies around in something resembling a dance. They don't want to come eat, but their parents, my brothers and sisters and their spouses, stop playing volleyball and wave them over, saying they won't get ice cream later if they don't eat now. They look temporarily annoyed and harried, but I think, I know, they're all happy in their good lives.

Lorraine and I squabbled sometimes, due mostly to her stubbornness, but it was always an adventure. She said our someday kids were bound to be crazy, just like the two of us, but we both kind of liked the idea.

Gigi Gran has made some remark that makes everybody laugh and my cousin Mae's got her arm around me and she's saying. "Yyyyy . . . yyyyy . . . yyyyou're doing great, Bob." She's smiling a little goofily, a piece of sweet corn stuck in her teeth. They're all looking at me now, the whole big bunch of them, even the uninvited neighbor with his bongos strapped around his waist, even Steve who's standing up now, wagging his tail expectantly. I'm in a panic, thinking I'm supposed to say something, but the neighbor saves me. He slaps the bongos and says, "Good God, let's eat!" And so. We do.

V.
Together, we can bury it.

WILD YELLOW DOG, GIANT RED FOX

The house is always quiet. The girl, named Millicent, is used to it. She is eight years old and this is all she remembers. She watches her mother, who stands holding a saucepan, at a loss.

"Mother?"

"I've forgotten what to do next. I don't know how to work any of this."

To Millicent, it is as if her mother is on camera. The mother hosts her own local television show exposing products that do not work as they are supposed to. Earlier, she taped a show where she demonstrated a stain remover that could not be properly aimed and that had a faulty pump action. She is funny on the show though in life she is quite grave. There was a man who used to come and visit and take Millicent's mother out to dinner, but he stopped.

"You are making the prune whip, remember?" The girl indicates the array of chopped, pitted prunes on the cutting board, spread out like bugs. "You need to cook those," she says. Her mother has on a melon-colored apron. Her sleeves are rolled to her elbows.

"I don't think we're ready to start yet, Mother," the girl says. "And I've not had any lunch."

"Are you asking for lunch?"

"Not that it matters. . . ." The girl wanted to bake cookies, but her mother insisted on the prune whip. And pumpernickel bread. How they love the bread machine!

Her mother puts down the pan and removes the apron. "Let's lie down, dear. Let's draw the drapes and have a lie-down. Do not be obdurate. Later we can do the cooking, I promise."

Her mother's lips are pale, as if they've been iced. The girl is used to her behavior. She would prefer to go outside and sit in the snow.

She has only one baby doll, named Helen. The doll's hair has been cut short and the plugs of plastic hair are visible where they enter its scalp. It wears a striped sailor dress and sits on the window ledge. Though she doesn't play with the doll, the girl enjoys its placid expression.

Her bedroom has a spiral staircase leading to a loft, where she sleeps. She requires few toys. There is a foosball table in the corner that belonged to her grandfather. Her mother feels the game would be better suited for a pub. The girl stands at the table, moving the plastic men back and forth with her hands, making them talk. She plays "family" with them even though the mother looks like the father and they both look like the baby.

At Christmas, her grandparents arrive. The grandmother is dressed in a red sweater dress with a fur scarf around her neck. Her boots are high-heeled Italian leather. The grandfather carries a shopping bag full of gifts. He asks for a cocktail. It is nine o'clock in the morning, but they have flown several hours to get there. He needs to smooth out the rough edges. The girl hugs him. She says, "I love you very much." He smells like coffee and sweat and heavy cologne.

The grandparents give her an old Royal type-writer.

"We'd like one letter per week, Millie. You can send it to our post office box in Florence," her grandmother says, and when Millicent asks what she should write about, her grandmother says anything at all, the spring rains, the holes in her socks. "It will help us not to miss you so much," she says. Before they leave, they tell the girl's mother she must buck up for the child's sake.

They record their adventures on a cassette re-corder the grandmother carries in her pocket. The girl hears her grandmother whisper, "Millie, listen carefully: We're standing before the Venus de Milo. It's a sort of statue. It is unutterably beautiful." There is noise and static and the tape goes quiet for a few seconds and the grandfather says something in an irritable tone the girl can't decipher.

They send cures from small foreign villages. Ground rosebud, if made into a poultice and slathered on the chest, will cure upon a single application, asthma. The girl's mother sniffs at the packets when they arrive, but never opens them.

"Millie, we are on the Left Bank, near the university, resting under a bright green umbrella. We are drinking something orange and syrupy. You would probably like it. We're just outside the site of a butcher's who ground up students and made from them a delicious sausage. This was a very long time ago so you mustn't worry. When we learn the name of this drink we will tell you it."

Millicent sends them stories about her father, whom she barely remembers. Her father died quickly of something horrible but this is never discussed. In the stories, her father is tall and kind and handsome, but he has two enemies: Wild Yellow Dog and Giant Red Fox. The animals live in dark corners of Millicent's bedroom.

There is a pause on the tape for traffic noise. The grandmother adds: "Please make your next story a happy one."

．　●　・

Helen is just fine the way she is, but the girl's mother wants to fix the doll. Or replace it. Someone is coming over to play today, the daughter of one of the mother's co-workers at the TV station.

"Maybe she will laugh at your dolly," the girl's mother says. "Let's put Helen in the closet for now."

Millicent has nervous habits, which worry her mother. She makes a constant pill-rolling action with her fingertips. Her mother is convinced she has Parkinson's disease. The girl agrees to put the doll's body in the closet. She screws off its head and sets it on her pillow.

She wants to please her mother, to make her smile. She cuts out the pictures of the girls in the newspaper fliers. The girls wear jaunty outfits or sparkling white underwear. In the advertisements, their mouths are open wide, as if they're laughing heartily. Maybe they're laughing because they've been caught in their underwear. The girls do not have asthma. They ride their bikes uphill into the wind.

The co-worker's daughter is tall, with a meaty, inscrutable face. She has brought a box of Mike and Ike's and a stuffed koala named Dick.

"Where's the ball for this?" she asks, flipping and shifting the rows of foosball men. It has started snowing again and everything in the girl's room has a grayish cast. Millicent hadn't realized the game even had a ball to it.

The co-worker's daughter bounces around the room, touching things, opening drawers.

"This is boring," she says and runs over and squeezes Millicent's cheeks hard. She notices the typewriter. There is a clean sheet of paper in it. She types: fifhghofasoawhehdglahakhwehrfogicxl

"This is stupid," she says. "I'm calling my mother."

Millicent rubs her face. "Go ahead. I want you to," she says. "It's dangerous here. You should take your friend and go," she says, picking the koala up off the floor.

Later, she hears the teakettle's slow whine gain strength and pitch until it's screaming. Why doesn't her mother remove it from the burner? She chews on Helen's rubbery arm. It tastes like dirt. Her grandparents want a new story, but she can't find the words. She climbs up to the old typewriter. There are purple smudges under her eyes. Wild Yellow Dog and Giant Red Fox slink in closer, eyeing her.

WHAT KIND OF PERSON GIVES SECRETS TO THE SKY?

Peter and Meggy and I are putting glasses of ice water on the tables. We work in the dining room at St. Anne's Home for Aged Nuns. They wheel the Sisters in around 4:30 for their dinner so they get them back to their rooms by six. Goodnight, nuns! I stop pushing the cart and sit down. Peter asks, "What's wrong?" One of the orderlies has parked Sister William in the corner, facing the wall. "I can't stand the smell of those Harvard beets," I tell him.

My mother is dating a guy named Gil, who works for the cable company, so now we have free cable. Last night, we watched "White Oleander" and my mom kept saying, "My God, Michelle Pfeiffer is gorgeous." Finally, Gil says, "I could take or leave her." He sucks the salt off the popcorn seeds and spits them back into the bowl.

When I was little, we used to go to Shell Rock to my uncle's farm. In the spring we'd get twenty-five-cent kites and stand in the middle of an open field and give them up to the wide blue sky. My dad scribbled on a piece of paper, tore it halfway and stuck it onto the string. After a few stutters, the paper hurried away from us, up the kite string, until we couldn't see it anymore. I asked him, was that a prayer? No, he said, it was a secret.

Peter's lucky. He gets to wear a white polo shirt and khakis. Of course he looks like a dork, but consider Meggy and I in our polyester pantsuits. Harvest gold. A-line top that zips right up the middle. The pants are flared and there's piping along the sides. Once, when we went to the Barley Corn after work, I changed in the backseat of my Vega. I wadded my uniform into a ball. Two days later, I found it underneath the seat and shook it out. No wrinkles.

When my mother asked, "Who's the father?" I looked her right in the eye and said, "I don't know." I'm not stupid. What is she going to say to that?

Peter says, "no shit" and Meggy's mouth drops open. She starts to laugh. We're eating roast chicken and vanilla pudding in the break room. "Tell me what's funny because I could use a laugh," I say. "You're grossing me out, by the way." Her front teeth are coated with pudding. It's dribbling down her chin. When she can finally speak, she says, "When did this happen? I mean you're always with us. Or at school." I hand her a napkin. What Meggy doesn't seem to know is that it only takes a minute to have sex. One minute.

The Barley Corn is this dive bar we discovered in Dike. You have to drive right out of Waterloo, out into the country until you get to the little farm towns. Dike has its own Main Street and bar after bar and nobody cards. We are sophisticated. We drink sloe gin fizzes. We roll our eyes at the selections on the jukebox. You got any real music?

My mother is a large woman. She's six foot tall and she's heavy. Not fat, just big all over. And pretty. I am small, like my dad. There is nothing pretty about me. Mr. Stebbins, my algebra teacher, tells me my hair is the color of wheat and that he knows I don't dye it because most girls, if they dyed their hair, would choose a nicer shade of blonde.

I've been dreaming about monkeys. Wild monkeys attacking me, scratching and clawing at me. Gil says don't eat pizza before going to bed. But that's all there is around here anymore. And another thing, does Gil live here now?

I was in the backseat of the car. We had a big car then, with wide vinyl covered seats with springs underneath. I was bouncing on the seat and waiting for my parents to yell at me to stop, but they didn't say anything. My mother was driving. We parked at the train station and she grabbed hold of my hand. Ouch, I said. My dad got a suitcase out of the trunk and knelt down and kissed me. I asked him how come the sky was white and he said that means snow is coming. I can still see it. His sad face, the bare trees, the white sky.

I love how the guy at the Barley Corn doesn't give me any shit when I order a sloe gin fizz. I'm just having the one anyway. "Are you tired?" Peter asks. "A little." Meggy's dancing with some guy to a country song. "We could go," Peter says. Peter lost his license and now he doesn't drink anymore. I pull the maraschino cherry off the plastic sword with my teeth and swallow it. "Shall we dance?"

My dad just shows up one day. I walk in the door and there he is, sitting with my mom at the kitchen table. My dad looks about a hundred years old. I drop my book bag and kick off my shoes. "Hey," I say. He stands up and looks at me and shakes his head. Who does he think he is?

Gil wants to know what I think of the name "Gunner." To be honest, I don't think much of it at all. Gunner! My mom has no opinion. There is only so much she can think about. She keeps asking when I'm going to cash that check, the one my dad left folded and set on its ends, like a tent, on my pillow. He'd written the words "good luck" on the memo line and underlined them. Twice.

I watched from the window as he got into his car. I thought if he waves, I'll wave back. But he only looked at me and lifted his fingers off the steering wheel, the way people do when they're just dashing out for a minute and you both know they'll be right back.

DAFFODIL

Some boys from Trinity stand in a group across the street. They have such shiny hair. They are brilliant. The skinny one waves to me. The sun slips behind them, behind the mountains. The skinny one cups his hands around his mouth. "Daaaaaaaphneeeeee," he yells. The other boys laugh. I cross and let my backpack slip off my shoulder. "Peace," I say and the Trinity boys, they are so fine, they say peace back.

"I've been seeing my father kissing some woman in his car when I'm walking home from basketball practice," I say. "Different spots, he changes it up. Scrawny woman, hair like fingers pointing out of her head. He can kiss whoever he wants, no question. But I'm tired, seriously tired, of these displays."

The Trinity boys don't blame me at all. They know I am not stupid about the world. I am a robust girl. Nevertheless, like everyone else I have limits. I am a clock that winds down.

"Check it," I say, because there they are, Jesus, right in the parking lot of Sunnyside Foods. Like he wants me to see him. The Trinity boys follow my finger. And the skinny one whistles. My father and the woman untangle themselves. I wave my arms and yell, "Over here, Hot Shot."

Every night my mom dreams she's sprayed with bullets. "I can feel the blood seeping from the holes," she says.

I want to scream. I want to tell her, Don't rock back and forth like that, don't affect that gypsy accent! Emotionally, my father is sixteen years old. The dream indicates all loss of hope.

I am the best freshman center in Terre Haute. My father sits in the bleachers at all the home games. He has saved every one of my baby teeth and carries them in a leather pouch. He has been known to show them to the other spectators. The night he moved out, he shot Nerf balls into the hoop on my bedroom door. I sat on the bed with my head deep in the hood of my sweatshirt, pretending to read *Cannery Row*. "I am at a crossroads, Daffodil," he told me. A crossroads!

I stop at Sunnyside and buy food for dinner. I am my mother's angel. I buy cigarettes and a Bic lighter. Those boys wait across the street. I'm going to offer them a smoke. The clerk counts change. He tells me to be good and shakes my hand. He doesn't care. Around here, I am a celebrity.

DISASSEMBLY

"You're the girl, aren't you?" the woman says.

I'm sidled up to the bar at the Knights of Columbus Hall. It's 11:00 in the morning on New Year's Eve and we've just buried my dad. I ask the bartender to splash some more rum into my drink. I call him "barkeep" like we're in a saloon. I'm the only one drinking, but I'm doing it for my dad. He insisted there be an open bar.

"I've been sitting right over there, trying to figure it out," the woman says. "The paper said he had seven sons and one daughter and I said to myself, I have got to see this poor girl."

She's short and squat, bedecked with a dozen or so necklaces and gold and silver chains. Her bosom stands between us like a very large Christmas present.

"It's Joy, right? The unmarried one."

With effort, I focus, but she's juddering like an old film reel.

"My name is Barbara Lee," she says. She looks at my right hand, the one holding the highball glass, and brushes crumbs from the corner of her mouth. "I didn't know your father at all. I just like coming to these things."

A small, male relative in a three-piece suit has been running rings around the buffet table. Now he's changed course and seems intent on tackling me. I step aside just in time and he barrels right into a loaded coat rack and is boomeranged back a few feet, landing on his back. Wailing ensues.

My nephew comes harumphing up, apologizing, lifting the kid to his feet. I press my palms to my aching head.

Barbara Lee is still yammering. On the other side of the hall, my oldest brother climbs up on a platform and waves his arms, calling out to the rest of us, the siblings, for a photo. It's because of me, the sister, the one who moved so far away, that we have to do this when we can. Even, and maybe especially, if someone has died.

"Say, where'd you get those necklaces?" I ask. "I want some."

She appraises my clothes: I dress like a communist.

"Walgreens. They're on sale."

"Will you take me?"

The barkeep pours the rest of my drink into a

Styrofoam cup and tops it up. Barbara Lee helps thread my arms through the sleeves of my coat.

She drives a vintage VW bug. Riding along with my shoulder practically touching a stranger's, I feel like someone who's been given a day pass.

"Do you want to talk?" she says. "You know. About your loss?"

"Nope."

"Oh that's a relief." She starts singing along to the song on the radio. It's an old Supremes song. "You know, this is just what I needed," she says. "Maybe it's weird, but I'm happy."

"I'm just sort of happy," I tell her.

The Walgreens is dilapidated and post-apocalyptic. Bins of discounted Christmas decorations and candy and gift sets ugly up the aisles. I keep my sunglasses on. Barbara Lee hustles ahead as I sip my rum and coke through a straw. I start to shiver again the way I did at the cemetery, as if I'm being disassembled.

I catch up to her in aisle ten. The bin of tangled necklaces resembles a snake pit. She extricates several and loops them over my head. I feel them there against my chest, lending me weight and substance and possible sparkle.

"Damn. These aren't really me," I say.

"Are you kidding?" she says. "These are everyone."

We find a mirror in the cosmetics aisle. Barbara Lee peers into it with me and all I can focus on is her round face, now registering vague disapproval. Back at the Knights of Columbus, my brothers have probably stopped wondering what happened to me. Maybe the thing is over by now. They have gathered up all the pictures and mementos of our dad's life and hauled them away.

I take off the necklaces and hand them to her. "I should get back."

I buy some Excedrin and she buys a Snickers and a marshmallow Santa and we sit in the car while she eats them.

"I'm sorry."

"Don't be sorry," she says. "It was a hoot."

She starts the car and there's more old Motown playing on the radio. She cranks the volume and I adjust the seat until I'm practically lying down. Barbara Lee and I sing along with Aretha in loud and fantastically off-pitch voices.

My brothers insist that I stand right in the center for all family photos. It is our custom. And one of them will say, *a rose among thorns*! And another will forget to put down his can of Bud. There's a very old photo of all of us scrunched together on the couch, the bare and dirty feet of the youngest ones sticking out at the camera. I'm the baby, sitting on my oldest brother's lap, arms outstretched, like Ta-Da!

BE MY, BE MY BABY

They sat close on the sofa, their feet propped on the coffee table. His right shoe touched her left shoe and his shoes were loafers and her shoes were ballerina flats. Neither one of them had very large feet and they decided their four propped feet resembled a family, a mom and a dad and their twin daughters. Darryl told Joyce again that he loved her shoes and asked again what kind of shoes they were.

On the mantle, a candle dripped onto a saucer and the walls shifted and shuddered in the flickering light. They'd been listening to the old songs she liked when she was a teenager but now the room was quiet.

"Drafty," he said. "This room."

"Yes." She sneezed into the crook of her arm like they showed on the public service announcements.

"I'd better skedaddle."

"Yes. Oh, would you like some milk?" He liked how soft her face looked, like the women on *Star*

Trek. They put Vaseline on the camera lens to make them look dreamy.

"Milk?" She jumped up and went to the kitchen, pulled a carton out of the fridge. She sniffed and winced. Curdled. "Never mind! I have olives." Her voice dropped. "And Maalox."

"It's okay. I don't like milk per se." It was nearly 11 o'clock. Around 9 o'clock he'd decided he loved every single thing about her. He rubbed his face with both hands and swung his legs to the floor. Oh, but really.

In the kitchen, Joyce was pulling everything out of her refrigerator, the olives, some curry paste, a half bottle of ketchup and a tub of margarine. She worked the little wire shelves out and tossed them into the sink, filled it with soapy water.

"Oof. I live like a pig," she shouted from the kitchen, which was only a few steps away. "Ha!" she added.

"I haven't had milk in forty years," Darryl said, but not loud enough for her to hear.

He stood and blew out the candle and watched her working, her back to him. A kind of vapor rose from the hot water all around Joyce that made her look exotic or very sweaty. He couldn't decide.

CANCER ARM

It's Thanksgiving and your mother appears and disappears at will. One second ago, she was touching your shoulder, whispering something funny. You think you might grab hold of her, bury your face in the folds of her neck, but you look up and she's gone. It's as if she's a vapor, sprayed from a can. She smells like Dove soap.

She keeps *The Big Book of Cancer Symptoms* on the coffee table. You can't fathom her guests happily leafing through it as she flies off to blend margaritas, yet there it sits, dwarfing *Rocky Mountain Sunsets: Complete with Poetry*, the book *you* gave her.

The book has diagrams you can follow, like a maze, starting with one symptom and then answering a series of questions, weaving your way down the page. Sometimes you're led off to one side where the book tells you, "This is the common cold." Or you're led all the way to the bottom of the page where it says "See your doctor immediately" in red letters. The pages are embossed with your mother's fingerprints.

It's Thanksgiving and you always sit next to your brother-in-law, Peter, who is easily the smartest one of the whole bunch, yet nobody listens to him. Undaunted, Peter keeps on talking. He always knows when you're lying, which is often. He's a sort of savant lie detector. You ask him to pass the peas. He asks why you're late. And you say, "phone call from an old friend" and he says, "bullshit" plucking a hair off your sweater and you say, "you're right! Please pass the buns."

Your mother listens to Deepak Chopra's books on tape. It is a project of hers. You always pronounce his name Choke-Ra and she corrects you. Deepak Chopra says you shouldn't think too much about cancer or you will get it.

Well then.

What your mother doesn't know is that you're terrified. You think about it all the time. Cancer cancer cancer. Cancer leg. Cancer arm. You've eaten too many cancer hot dogs and sausages in your life. You've gotten too many cancer sunburns. Cancer throat. Cancer head. Too much cancer sex.

Your thoughts have the power to change the structure of your cells, cancerizing them. You can feel it and it rattles you.

It's Thanksgiving and you are six years old. Your knee socks are pulled up over your kneecaps. Rusty, your Golden Retriever, is under the table and now and then you drop a piece of turkey on the floor for him. What you'd really like is a Tollhouse cookie or some muskmelon, cut into chunks. You think Rusty's distended stomach is from eating too much, though in truth, he hardly eats at all. He won't make it to Christmas and neither will your father. Everyone knows this but you.

You cheated on your husband one month after you were married. Peter knows, but he doesn't judge. How you love Peter!

He leans over, says, "How are you, Doll?" and you want to say, "I'm hurting. I can't sleep. All food tastes like old cheese and I'm alarmed." Instead you tell him that you're splendid. And he says, "You're not" and you imagine the word *biopsy* floating between the two of you, in bubble letters.

The word sounds happy to you, almost drunken. Biopsy is whimsy's first cousin. It is a daisy chain wrapped around the neck of a child. Who could worry over something so pretty?

It's Thanksgiving and your mother's house has gone golden and clotted with voices. There are all these people. Your sister, Kate, and Peter. Your uncles who never married, Uncle Fred who served in Nam and Uncle Brian who still pulls quarters out of your ears and the neighbor couple, Martin and Marie, who come every year because they have no family of their own. There's way too much food and the table's crowded and you'd still rather have a cookie or a wiener on a bun or a bowl of oatmeal than the slabs of steaming turkey breast, the out-sized mounds of mashed potatoes. You have always hated this meal. You catch yourself leaning down to touch Rusty's head, and this makes you laugh and cry at the same time.

Your mother waits for you to lean back so she can set down a plate of sweet potato pie. Exasperated, she flutters away, but you catch her wrist, draw her hand to your lips and kiss it, just in time.

TAILS

Lon's tired and cranky, like a child, even rubbing his eyes with a curled fist. A shock of hair stands up on the back of his head and he doesn't want to be at the mall anymore but in front of his TV, drinking a beer. He'd asked me what I wanted for Christmas and I told him a black and white kitten, but I notice we have not visited any pet stores.

I try to tell him I hadn't gotten the administrative assistant job I was vying for. I thought I was a shoo-in. He says, somebody else will take you, and rubs at his eyes. People are moving slowly, like they've been shopping their entire lives and they can't find the exit. I want a pretzel and something cold to drink. Lon stops dead in the middle of the mall and a sea of loping shoppers part around him. He appears to be watching their feet.

I say, "Somebody else will take me? Lon, do you realize how awful that sounds? You're making me feel worse."

"You know, people say it's the beautiful things that break the heart: verdant hillsides, placid, melty sunsets over the ocean, the impossible delicate fingers of newborns. That's wrong- headed. Those things are a blessing. And your disappointment is just a disappointment."

"I love you, Lon, but goddamnit."

I leave him standing there and purchase my snack, debate mentally whether to go back or to just go straight out to the parking lot. But Lon looks haggard and I am his ride home, so I go back. I show him my enormous pretzel. He makes a face. "I know," I say. Traffic moves in both directions on either side of us. A woman pushing one of those double strollers mutters as she passes by. I can smell the Greek chicken from the food court and wish I'd gotten that instead.

Lon's not moving. I ask him if we're done shopping. I pick a penny up off the floor. Tails. Shit. If he got me the kitten, I would name it Rousseau because it sounds cool and elevated, like from another realm.

"You want to know what breaks my heart?" He says. "It's perfectly white cushioned-soled running shoes on the feet of 80-year-old men. The kind meant for marathons. Oh Christ. Get me a gun."

Lon's eyes have an uncertain, glazed look to them. He's 40 but old for his age, with some kidney complaint he won't talk about. I loop my arm around his baggy shoulders, drip some mustard sauce on his sleeve. I tell him it's okay, that he's right, and that I will set my sights on something else, something less stellar, but that the fingers of babies do break my heart, beautiful as they are. And he's nodding, going okay, okay.

WAKE UP

My neighbor, Mr. Dorn, is standing naked on my front steps, singing. He looks like a reptile in the moonlight. Maybe he's sleepwalking, in which case, I know not to go and shake him or he'll keel over with a heart attack. I've read about this.

This is my third night of insomnia and I'm feeling as close to crazy as I ever have. Lack of REM sleep can lead to hallucinations and disordered thinking. It's possible Mr. Dorn is not even here, but cozy in his bed with Mrs. Dorn. It's possible I'm not even here.

I go to the kitchen and heat up some leftover pumpkin soup. Mr. Dorn is singing "My Cherie Amour" and is on the "la la la" part. He doesn't sound anything like Stevie Wonder.

Bill, my cat, rubs against my leg and I crumble off bits of bread and cheese and she eats it out of my hand, taking her time. Bill misses my husband, the one she really loved. The one who really loved her.

The apartment he moved into doesn't allow cats. That last night he held Bill's face close to his and said, "This is only temporary," but that was news to me.

Mr. Dorn is having difficulty reaching the high notes. Bill jumps to the windowsill and hisses at him.

"Bill, come on. Don't be a bitch." I pick her up and rub her under her chin, the way she likes. Mr. Dorn finishes the song and stands holding his penis, looking amazed, as if penises had just been invented and he'd been asked to try this one out for size.

I don't want to call and scare Mrs. Dorn. They are such a nice couple. Just before Christmas, Mrs. Dorn was going away to some craft fair in Minneapolis and she knew Mr. Dorn would be lonely so she built him a snow version of herself standing in front of their house. It was a helluva stacked snow woman. Mrs. Dorn used some artistic license. I took a picture of Mr. Dorn standing next to "Darla II" and made an 8x10 of it for him to frame. He cried when I gave it to him and she'd only been gone three days.

I call my husband sometimes in the middle of the night.

"Are we going to be okay?" I ask, whispering. I don't want to wake him up completely. I read somewhere that people in a semi-conscious state are incapable of lying.

Mr. Dorn needs to wake up and go home to his bed. I push up the window and lean close to the screen and start singing, "La la la la la la."

He blinks. "La la la la la la." He clears his throat and lets go of his penis. Mr. Dorn and I are singing "My Cherie Amour" together. Maybe he's still asleep or maybe he's not, but I'll say this, the two of us are really something.

BLOOMS

Dan the neuropsychologist wants to test Nona's personality. Nona is Dan's research assistant. They work together in a large university hospital. Every day he asks her to talk about her boyfriend. This, she resists. She feels it would be untoward, like presenting a case at Grand Rounds. The neuropsychologist wants details and supporting arguments, some factual account. She hasn't the energy for it.

Nona observes Dan's pale green eyes widen whenever he speaks to their boss, the department chair. His speech becomes formal and direct. The department chair closes his eyes as if he's listening through headphones. Nona is not personally qualified to speak to the department chair.

She's in the conference room reading a paperback when Dan enters. His face resembles a self-portrait of Van Gogh. He gives her the personality inventory and a #2 pencil and sits on the rug like a kindergartner. He laughs and hangs his head in his hands and sighs deeply.

He says, "Nona my daughters—do you know how much I love them?"

"A lot. What are their names again?"

"Thomas and Greg. We chose not to burden them with societal norms and expectations."

Nona knew this, she just wanted to hear it again. Later, she'll climb under the quilts with Bill, her boyfriend and whisper this into his ear, hoping to make him laugh.

This afternoon, she's scheduled to test Patient RD. She sees him over a period of three days every six months. His actual name is Ray Dripps, but in the textbooks he's referred to as RD. In neuropsychology circles, RD is considered a celebrity. He got sick after riding the Screaming Terror at Busch Gardens when he was fifteen. He vomited all over his friend's Camaro, then went home and slept for twenty-four hours. He woke up with a spectacular headache.

RD's chief problem is that he perseverates. He's incapable of changing mental sets. He carries a flashlight and flicks it on and off. When Nona administers the neuropsychological exams, she asks him a number of questions, to which he answers, "I don't give a rat's ass." His photo, in the medical journals, shows a man with a mild, expressionless face and one hand raised, palm out, as if he's taking an oath.

She plays a card-sorting game with him in which the rules constantly change. RD has a genius IQ yet this game confounds him. She tells him, "It's okay, really. This game is tough. It's exactly like life, my man."

"Yes, thank you," he says and bursts into tears. He leans over and kisses her knee. In his chart, she writes *emotionally labile*.

The exam room is roughly the size of a walk-in closet. There are no windows. Nona is not allowed to dress it up. Bill gave her one of those glass-sipping birds when she got the job, but she can't have it in here. It sits next to the coffee maker in the conference room. It swings forward and sips from a mug. The sipping bird wears a top hat and a bow tie. Nona thinks the patients might enjoy it.

She feels boxy inside her clothes today. She feels unwieldy and outsized, like a hedgehog, in her lab coat. In reality, she's very thin. She's a minnow. RD is sullen and uncooperative. She finishes the game and forgoes the other standardized tests, the memory tests, the language batteries. She needs to run out her time with him, so instead she writes her grocery list. Her boyfriend's needs are simple: chicken pot pies and baking potatoes and Quaker Oat Squares.

Gold's medicated powder. Minted dental floss. Also, he drinks one whole gallon of milk per day. She writes it all down. Out of the corner of her eye, she notices that RD is rubbing his crotch, looking at her legs. They really need the sipping bird in here.

After work, Nona takes the Ride-On bus to Hy-Vee and buys the food and walks home with two bags in each hand and her purse slung across her chest. She wears a pea coat and a stocking cap. She and Bill live in a log cabin duplex at the top of Dodge Street behind Home Town Dairy. A line of refrigerator trucks are parked, motors running, all night, but she's never seen them go anywhere. Also, she's never seen any cows. Where are the cows? Ahead, the side of the duplex that she and Bill share is dark like an eye with a patch.

She lets herself in and turns on the lights. The bookcase in the center separates the living room and the bedroom. Bill's a lump on the waterbed, which takes up every last inch of the room. She has to crawl along the edge of it to get to the bathroom door. Bill rises and falls on a wave.

"I'm unwell," she says, turning on the fluorescent light over the bathroom sink. She splashes her face with water, scoops some into her mouth.

Bill shifts under the quilts. "I read today," he says. "*The Biophysics of Archery and the Archer.*"

Nona crawls onto the bed and pulls the quilts away from his face. "Liar."

"It was fascinating."

The man who lives on the other side of the duplex nailed a target to the cottonwood tree and practices archery every day. Even in December, he's out there practicing. For a while, they referred to him as William Tell. This was when every morning Nona and Bill left the log duplex together to get coffee, to go to their jobs, when they rode in the rusted Vega together and laughed about their neighbor. When Bill was himself.

"Do you know," Nona says, "there's a bucket beside the secretary's desk full of formaldehyde? Do you know what's inside it, floating around in all that preservative?" She runs her fingers along Bill's brow to his cheekbone. "Can you guess?"

"I hate guessing."

"This will amuse you. Guaranteed."

Bill groans and rolls over, away from her.

"Hey. Come on, we were talking."

On the other side of the duplex, she hears music. Something old and familiar that her brother used to play. Three Dog Night. She smells onions and tomatoes cooking. The neighbor man belts out, "Joy to the world," then, "shit."

Nona rolls off the bed. "I'll fix you something."

She pierces a potato and the frozen crust of a

pot pie with a fork and puts them both in the tiny oven. She pulls the personality inventory from her bag and sits in front of the oven with a blanket over her legs.

I like to torture small animals. T or F?

It's entirely too easy to guess what they're after. Nona considers answering the questions to make Dan the neuropsychologist think she's a paranoid schizophrenic. Or suffering from some rare, yet elegant psychosexual disorder. Dan has a wife named Chris. Thomas and Greg are very little. Dan put his hand on Nona's shoulder once, in the exam room. He rubbed her collarbone with his thumb.

The wall clock sounds like raindrops on tin and on the other side of the duplex, the archer whoops and says, "God damn." Bill struggles out of the bed. Nona hears him peeing.

Sometimes I feel I am the Christ. True.

Bill comes and warms his palms by the oven.

Nona says, "Hey, this is weird. Everything's amplified. Even my own voice, right now. I think I'm running a fever, but I'm so cold."

"That's odd."

"Have you guessed?"

"What?"

"In the bucket. Okay, I'll tell you. It's a human *brain.*" She nods. "There's a brain in a bucket by the secretary's desk. A *mop* bucket."

"Oh Christ, that's awful." Bill crumples onto the sofa. "That's horrific. Why on earth did you tell me that?"

Bill's belly is a drum on his lap. She'd like to thunk it with her index finger, hear it reverberate. It's one bowlful of melancholy he's got there. Six months ago, she hurt him by sleeping with another man. But Bill's funk had been in place long before she had drinks with the graduate student and ended up not coming home that night. Nona tells herself this, but she is not absolutely sure it is the case.

So every night she tries to fix this one horrible mistake. To show him. See? She's not going anywhere! See how she makes dinner and tells interesting stories?

Everything in the town before the first snow is colored an expectant silver-gray. The hospitals and clinics, the lecture halls, and dormitories huddle, watchful like old men. Nona sold the Vega and now she takes the Ride-On bus with the college students. When the bus passes over the bridge, she closes her eyes. The river churns beneath her, the color of nickels. Every morning, there is the collective breath of the students, fermented and sweet. And the blind man who sits directly behind the driver, who runs his fingers through his hair and licks them.

At the office, Dan and the secretary are leaning in, looking at the brain. The bucket sits on the secretary's desk. The reception area smells like Nona's high school science lab.

"It's smaller than I expected," the secretary says.

"Everybody says that," Dan tells her. "The seat of consciousness is not much bigger than a grapefruit. Nona—wow. Did you sleep at all last night?"

"How'd she die?" the secretary asks.

"Hanged herself." Dan touches the brain with his index finger.

The secretary nods. "It's kind of cheerful the way it bobs around like that. It reminds me of Christmas. I'm sorry, but it's true."

Nona pulls off her pea coat and replaces it with her lab coat. She'd tested this patient over a period of twelve months. The woman had a stroke and suffered from word deafness. She believed everyone around her had begun to speak in code. She presented with generalized anxiety disorder and paranoia. Nona thought this was a pretty reasonable response. In testing sessions, she passed the woman notes: *Trust me. I am your friend.*

"Here," Nona says. She gives Dan the personality test. "Finished."

"Why didn't you stay home this morning? You didn't want to stay home? You should see yourself. We're not supposed to bring germs into this place."

"I'm fine. I'll be fine."

"No, you should go."

"Nope. Staying."

There's a stain on Dan's white shirt. Nona wonders if it's the same one he wore yesterday.

"Let Bob take care of you. You know, for a change."

"Bill."

The secretary lifts the handle of the bucket. Some of the formaldehyde splashes over the edge onto her skirt. She sets the bucket on the floor and covers it with a towel. "Probably the smell is what's making you sick," she says. "It's getting to me, too."

"I thought someone from neurobiology would have picked it up from now. Why do we still have it?" Nona asks.

The secretary shrugs. Dan walks off waving the personality test. "I'll have your results this afternoon. Oh the mysteries of Nona!"

RD's bored with the memory tests. He aces them anyway. Nona says, "Remember those six words I gave you earlier? Do you remember them? RD, what were those six words?"

"I don't give a rat's ass."

"Wrong," she says.

In a pocket in the back of RD's chart are copies of his brain scans. CAT scans, MRIs, and PET scans. Nona takes them out. She doesn't usually. She's not supposed to.

"You want to see these?" She holds them up to the light. He takes them from her.

"Those look like flowers," RD says. "Like blooms."

Dan and the department chair are talking right outside the door. The department chair is from Lisbon. He presents with authority at Grand Rounds. He shows the scans on an overhead projector and points to the focal lesions that explain everything. Much can be learned about brain function from those who are damaged. They are our expeditionary guides. If Dan and the department chair come in now Nona will probably get into trouble.

"Are you giving them your brain, RD? You know, when you die?"

"Peonies. Maybe they look like peony blooms. No. Chrysanthemums."

RD examines the scans. He lifts them to his face, one by one. "Chrysanthemums are the favored flower for homecoming corsages. Chrysanthemums are an autumn blooming flower, that's why. Of course, peonies are always covered with ants."

"You shouldn't. They cut your head open with a saw. It's horrific."

Outside the door, Dan stops talking when the department chair sneezes, then sneezes twice more.

"I'd better put these away now," Nona says. RD's looking at his PET scan, tracing the fluted edges of his cortex. He won't give it to her.

"Gray blooms," he says.

"You can change your mind. Even if you signed something. It's okay to change your mind." But this is not his strong point.

He's about to cry. He's shoving the scan into the pocket of his chart and his hands are trembling. It's gone quiet outside the examination room.

"Hey now," Nona says. "Don't, don't." She means to pat RD's hand, but raises her fingertips to touch his broad, shining forehead, the skin that covers his skull.

Bill calls at lunchtime.

"I just wanted to hear your voice."

"You've had a rough morning?"

"Yeah." He starts to say something else, but he doesn't. He doesn't love her. Why does he stay? She experiences a sudden, blinding desire to go home and kick his ass. The Home Town Dairy cows live quite placidly on a farm, of course. Many miles away.

Dan's passing out flyers to the staff as they leave for the day. He and his band are playing tonight at The Mill. Mostly covers of John Prine. It is their first gig, but he's acting confident. The Mill specializes in spaghetti with a choice of sauces. It's very cheap.

"You have to come," he tells Nona.

"Who's John Prine?"

Dan stares at her. "Okay, that's it. You really have to come."

He pulls Nona into the conference room, pours coffee.

"Shouldn't you be going?"

He looks at his watch. "I have some time. Anyway," he says. "This?" He's got a printout of her test results. They sit down.

"I'm weary, Dan. I'm not kidding."

"It's bogus anyway. *Somebody* did a little horsing around."

"Just get to know people the normal way why don't you."

The secretary pops in to unplug the coffee maker and say good-bye. "You don't look a bit better," she says to Nona. "In case you didn't know, it's snowing."

They hear her go around flicking off the lights. On the white board, the department chair has drawn a crude representation of a diseased amygdala. It looks like an almond.

Dan's tapping his pencil on the table. "Come and hear us play tonight."

Nona's whole body aches. "I just want to go home."

On their first date, Bill took Nona to hear a string quartet in the music department. They were both still students. After, they bought hot dogs from a street vendor and sat eating them on the stone wall surrounding her dormitory, swinging their legs like children. She asked him if he was having a good time. You're the best thing I know, he said. You're the best thing I'll ever know. She laughed, loving the wide-open admiration in Bill's eyes and said, well, maybe wait and see first.

Nona takes her Tupperware bowl out of the mini fridge in the conference room. It is a good-sized bowl. The leftover salad inside is covered in fur. The bowl takes some scrubbing before it's clean. She runs the water until it's scalding and rinses the bowl four times. She lifts it to her nose and smells it, then dries it with a paper towel.

The hallway is dim. She has to feel around for the light switch in the reception area. She kneels down and pulls the towel away from the bucket and winces from the smell. Carefully, she dips the Tupperware bowl into the formaldehyde. The brain bobs away slightly at first, then swims in with the liquid streaming into the bowl.

The Ride-On bus arrives late and empty. Nona takes a seat and places the bowl on her lap. The contents slosh around like soup. She wraps her arms around the bowl and holds it to her chest. She is shivering.

The driver looks at her in the rearview mirror and says, "Long day, huh?"

Nona looks out at the steady, slow falling snow. She wishes the bus weren't lit inside. It lumbers across the bridge and past the university buildings. A couple of students are pelting each other with snowballs outside a bar. Nona hears a thin stream of Christmas carols from the driver's radio. She grips the bowl tighter. The bus continues up Dodge Street to the dairy and her stop.

The duplex is bright on both sides tonight. She can see it through the snow. She's sure Bill is there, right now, awake and smiling and ready to receive her. As the bus draws nearer to the stop, Nona believes she can make out Bill's form through the snow and clouds of exhaust from the Home Town Dairy trucks. He is standing out there without a coat. It is as if he knows. Nona stands up. The motion of the bus sends her forward. She has to grab onto a seat back, catch her balance. But he's there, she's certain that's him, standing under the light.

The bus stops.

"Okay, Miss, you take it easy now," the driver says. But she is already down the steps and out, ankle deep in snow.

The bus pulls away from the curb. Nona wants

to run, but she might slip. That must be Bill waiting for her. She calls out to him, but the snow swallows her voice. She is breathless to tell him. I have quit my job. I have stolen the brain. And together, we can bury it.

Kathy Fish's short fiction has appeared in *Indiana Review, The Denver Quarterly, New South, Quick Fiction, Guernica* and elsewhere. She guest edited Dzanc Books' *Best of the Web 2010*. She has published two other collections of short fiction: a chapbook in *A Peculiar Feeling of Restlessness: Four Chapbooks of Short Short Fiction by Four Women* (Rose Metal Press, 2008) and *Wild Life* by Matter Press, 2010.